LADY MISTLETOE BY MIDNIGHT

JUDITH LYNNE

JUDITH LYNNE

ISBN: 978-1-953984-39-5 (E-book)

BOOKS BY JUDITH LYNNE

<u>Lords and Undefeated Ladies</u>

Not Like a Lady

The Countess Invention

What a Duchess Does

Crown of Hearts

He Stole the Lady

No Titled Lady

Lady Mistletoe by Midnight

<u>Maids Done Waiting</u>

The Lord Trap

The Lady Escape (Forthcoming)

<u>Cloaks and Countesses</u>

The Caped Countess

The Clandestine Countess

The Curious Countess

The Castaway Countess (Forthcoming)

<u>Ladies' Own Bakery</u>

The Regency romance comedy serial

DISCLAIMER AND GENTLE WARNINGS

This is a work of fiction and as such, its characters, events, words, and places are the product of the author's imagination.

This is a sweetly spicy Christmas book but does mention struggles with food, parent death, and terrible parenting. If this isn't your cup of tea today, I mention it so you may peacefully pass this by.

PREFACE

MY DEAR READERS,

So many books I bring you have connections between their characters, it was inevitable that one day I would bring you a book with none.

While a most elegant and well-regarded bookshop did exist at the same time that might seem to be a model for the one in this book, mine is purely fictional, I assure you.

The Treaty of Ghent—and the love our characters find within these pages—is, however, real.

Your obedient servant,

Judith Lynne

CHAPTER 1

*J*enny, *leave.*

If Isabel could only say the simple thoughts that crossed her mind. Polite society—which meant her mother—demanded Isabel blunt her sharpest thoughts.

And most of them were sharp.

Her mother wasn't here. None of her family lived here, in this bare little upper-story room in a faintly more respectable building than the boarding house down the street.

They had tucked her in this London closet, far away from their village and the risk of affecting her sister's chances of marriage. Like a cracked teacup that couldn't be used but which one couldn't bear to throw away.

In fact they were likelier to keep the teacup closer.

"Jenny, do leave me and start for home." Her mother wasn't here, and Jenny did not respond to hints. "You don't want to miss any of your Christmas Eve."

The maid dried her hands, looking at her mistress with dark eyes full of pity. It burned a bit, to be pitied by her own maid. Isabel's family required her to keep her thoughts veiled, yet the poverty of her situation—one chair, one small table, one little iron basket for firewood—was painfully apparent.

Her parents weren't poor. They simply did not want her to have callers.

"Leave you alone with a cold supper on Christmas Eve? What would my granny say?" Jenny tucked up a lock of hair as if her granny were watching.

Someday Isabel would be free of this never-ending circle of watching women.

Jenny's lock of hair fell often, with her vigorous sweeping and washing of linens. Isabel wished she had a lock of hair that free.

Perhaps freedom could begin right here and now with a little friendly conspiracy.

"Your gran will never know," said Isabel with a serious nod. "Go help her cook. I'll want to hear about Bill's new dog. I hope Frank and Caleb don't spend an hour fighting over the goose liver. Go! And tell me the stories on Monday. Tomorrow is not only Christmas, it's your half-day." Isabel's family might have put her away, but Jenny had a large boisterous family of her own.

Isabel had bread enough to last till the bakery opened again on Monday; she'd toast her little slab of cheese by the fire.

She had a little left of her month's allowance, but she did not intend to spend it on meat.

Jenny looked at her with big pitying eyes but Isabel urged her into her coat, then out the door.

Then the solitary lady of the house—well, *room*—waited impatiently, counting out ten minutes, to be sure Jenny had gone down all the flights of stairs and away down the street, where sounds of passing revelers grew louder second by second.

Isabel intended to join them.

She might be unmarried and unwanted, but she had the key to her own door. For the rest of her Christmas Eve and through Christmas, she had the freedom of being alone.

And she'd decided three months ago, over a dinner of parsnips and tea, to indulge herself in one frivolous thing. Just one.

She'd decided to celebrate Christmas by buying herself a book.

* * *

Victor threw the newspaper with enough force to make its rag pages *crack* against the carriage wall, then flop to the empty seat. Still the words of the foreign report floated before his eyes.

No progress

Unsure

Conversations ongoing

They were more tepid than his father's words for him—*weak, limp, useless*—but in the same vein. He'd wasted six months of work.

Just to come back here.

When the letter had reached him in Ghent, ragged and stained from its travels across a war-torn continent, Victor's impulse had been to ignore it. His father had spent a lifetime thinking him good for nothing; he'd spend his death thinking the same thing. Victor wished to stay in Ghent with his work.

But his friend Goulburn had recently married, and it had turned him sentimental. "You must go. A man deserves his son at his side when he dies."

Perhaps that was true, but if so, it was just another way Victor had failed.

"Beg yer pardon, Lord Hartwick, but have ye settled on yer direction?" the driver called down through the slot at his feet.

And now for the rest of his life, Victor would be called by his father's name.

He retrieved the hat he'd sent flying when he'd thrown the paper. "Stop anywhere. Stop here."

He ought to have been more polite. Mr. Bottle, the driver, was at least civil.

But after days spent cramped in carriages and ship's cabins, Victor needed to move, to breathe fresh air that did not smell of disappointment.

Well, this was London. It would be air, at any rate.

His boots thumped to the pavement before the carriage wheels even stopped rattling. The air had less snap than the low country December he'd left behind. Here it felt soft and smelled of rain.

"Head home, Bottle. Haven't you got children?"

Taken aback, the driver blinked his meaty eyelids. "Six, m'lord. Kind of ye to remember. But how will ye return?"

He'd rather sleep on the pavement than go back to Hartwick House, full of his father's servants all glaring and lurking in dark corners and behind cupboard doors.

Victor was a grown man; he'd traveled to Ghent at the request of an under-secretary of Parliament. He didn't need anyone's approval.

Just some fresh air free of glares for an hour or two.

"I'll engage a cab, Bottle, never fear. I'll find my way home." As the driver nodded and snapped the reins, horses lurching the carriage away, Victor muttered, "Whether anyone likes it or not."

His father's carriage disappearing in the wet air and busy

traffic, Victor walked on, feeling alone with his thoughts for the first time since his father had died.

He stalked from window to window, following the flickering orange light of candles through the gray glass panes of shops.

There were more candles than he expected, and suddenly, more shouts.

Ahead, a clump of men leaped against each other, red-faced, shouting.

Victor grabbed one sweating man by his sleeve. "Is it the treaty?" In a burst of hope, his eyes scoured every wall for handbills and the pavement round his feet. Perhaps a special edition of the news had been printed.

"Treaty?" The man looked pitying. "No, sir. It's Christmas Eve."

Christmas Eve?

The night meant nothing to him but some dim memories of bonfires in the country he'd seen as a child. There people had celebrated Christmas; not his father. His father had not celebrated anything but strength.

"Get up that tree, boy." He'd wave at an oak older than their family pedigree, and wait till Victor fell out.

Then he just stood there, the grim curve of his mouth curling downward in puzzled disgust.

The sweaty man before him now looked more puzzled than disgusted. Victor realized he still gripped the man's sleeve, and let him go.

Teeth clenched, Victor stalked on.

* * *

FREEDOM, decided Isabel, tasted like cold dust and chilled her nose.

Others might not care for it, but she found it bracing. Freedom need not be beautiful, only hers for a little while.

For better or worse, once she joined the traffic on the pavement her solitude was washed away in a flood of people. When she passed windows, she heard banging pots and shrieks, whether of pain or delight she could not tell; she was surrounded by the cacophony of shoe leather, wheels, and shouts. It was a hurricane of people.

Isabel preferred quiet, but her little room took it too far.

After all, what if this winter was like last? Nearly a year past, the south country had been mummified in heaping snowdrifts and fog. She'd spent months in her family's home, and the constant requirement to be quiet and unnoticeable had nearly driven her out of her senses.

It was right to take air whenever one could.

At the same time, every passing brush made her gasp and clutch at her purse. The weight of the little reticule was the result of months of planning, but executing the plan might take more nerve than Isabel had in reserve.

Nerve, she heard her father's voice say, *is just being more determined than the other fellow.*

He often said it, including to her suitors, perhaps trying to jog them into making the appropriate gestures. He never said it *to* Isabel; but she couldn't help hearing it.

If all this journey took was to be more determined than *past* Isabel, today she would do it.

It was far jollier to stroll past men in serious hats, ruffians in dirty caps, families trooping through the streets for their holiday, than to sit by a little stove listening to it all happen in the distance.

London was a bigger world than her village home. It would be her fault if her world stayed small.

Her mother often wrote how small her world *ought* to be.

Every letter closed with the exhortation that Isabel must never venture out without a suitable chaperone.

But her mother wasn't here.

In pockets along the street, girls Isabel's age—young women—gathered under the watchful eye of someone's mama; but they weren't looking at each other. They smiled quite openly at passing men in sailcloth trousers, men from the ships returning from war. They glanced fetchingly at gentlemen in stovepipe hats and battered neck ruffles who walked with canes, likely wounded abroad. And at any man in uniform, even if his hair were silvering.

Every marriageable woman in town wanted to snare one of the last possible husbands trickling back from Europe.

Isabel wondered if her mother had stashed her here in London as a last resort. Did she think London stuffed with eligible bachelors likely to take an interest in Isabel based on a passing glance? It wasn't.

Nor was it a small country town celebrating Christmas quietly with chestnuts and songs.

Plenty of the passing men hunched against the cold, going about their business with the same sour expressions they wore every other day. But plenty more veered drunkenly around the pavement, their clothes lurching one direction as they lurched another.

Occasionally painted ladies leaned out their open windows and laughed. That might be for Christmas or it might not.

Isabel did not veer. Her goal was Allenby's bookshop. Nothing unsavory would happen to her so long as her feet moved in that direction.

Not that she was entirely sure of the direction.

This might be the wrong street. Perhaps she shouldn't be here, seeing these people do these things.

She kept her small steps quick and tried not to stare.

One man spit a stream of foul brown liquid to the paving stones at her feet. Freezing, not even breathing, Isabel did not look up.

The moment forced a storm of competing requirements to settle in her head the way lightning left glass in the sand. She *was* the sort of brazen woman who walked abroad alone. If she could do that, she could give in to the impulse that made her the girl no one wanted to marry.

She met the spitting man's eyes, frowned, and shook her head *no*.

Taken aback, the big ham of a man actually shuffled back a few steps and muttered "Sorry m'm" before swinging around Isabel to take himself and his greasy waistcoat away.

Heart pounding, Isabel went on with lighter steps and a higher head. She might not be able to talk to people, but she could *talk back* and still survive. It was not the earth-shattering crime her family said.

Not that she'd talked.

It felt different now to see country families strolling together, joking and pointing at things in shop windows. Were those women like her, or not? Isabel wondered if they ever talked back.

The very existence of other country women made her feel more at home, but also a little hollow. They had a place in their family party, a group goal of finding different lives in lofty London.

It was odd that she was here to see them. Isabel had never expected to live in London. She'd expected a quiet life in a little house far from the city; a curate's house near an ancient church would have been ideal. A particular curate's house, one Isabel had passed every week all her life on her way to church. Isabel had never expected luxury.

But neither had she expected Mr. Ball to marry his cousin's school friend.

Or for Mr. Wheelock, Isabel's second choice, to marry his distant cousin. It was shocking how much damage a few too many words could do.

She had not expected to face a life with no home of her own, no husband, no children. Nor to be sent away to improve the chances of her younger sister marrying.

In fact, a number of things in life had surprised her badly.

The life ahead might be long and lonely, but Isabel could still walk. She could venture out to Allenby's, the famous bookseller near St. James' Square, and find it on her own two feet.

And here it was.

Holding on to her determination, her nerve, Isabel pushed open the squat brown door. Its bell made her jump.

But there was nothing to feel alarmed about. Inside she found a spacious little cavern of books, right in the heart of the city, stacked and stacked with heaps of treasure in the form of books.

She also hadn't expected to feel this much excitement.

A harried shopkeeper with messy hair—or had he dressed it that way on purpose?—bustled up to her in his black coat. She wondered if he actually ran the presses. "Yes, madam?"

She only wanted to get past him to the books. "A Christmas Eve book," she stammered, unable to string together a sentence with all the trimmings of polite but unnecessary words. She'd just come a long way. She had little boldness left.

He peered down over a disapproving nose. "If madam wishes to purchase a book, please inform me of your selection. It will be bound however you wish, delivered if you wish to pay the fee, or," here he examined her coat with obvious and insulting judgment, "you may stop in for it."

"I cannot take it with me? But the books." She could not

find many words of her own, but his made no sense. There were stacks of volumes on shelves and every table.

He grew frostier. "Madam, this is not Lackington's rag shop."

She did not know what that was, and wondered if she should have gone there.

The outer world was just as full of disappointment as one within doors, Isabel decided. Still, she'd come this far. Determination might not get her the immediate satisfaction of a book tonight, but she *would* have her book.

And she'd have her shopping excursion, and the excitement of not knowing what story she'd find, or what would happen next.

CHAPTER 2

A handbill snapped Victor out of his reverie, but it was not nailed to any shop's wall. It was printed by press, balanced on an easel inside the gray window next to a candle.

The etching on the bill was of a gentleman, lean and severe like himself, in a tall hat, among many volumes of bound books, hand outstretched to a spinning globe.

BOOKS
Good, substantial, and luxur-
ious bindings of all kinds
MAP FOLIOS
Fiction and history of every branch
Quarto and octavo, as req.
Enquire within

That was the sort of gentleman he might be. Not like his louche father, indulging his every desire. Surely lords could be circumspect of thought and deed.

The impulses he sometimes felt said otherwise. He found the handbill reassuring.

It drew him in; opening the door caused a sweet tinkle of a bell completely at odds with his mood and the violent sweep of his cape.

"How may I serve you, sir?"

As Victor swept in from the dank London air, a shopkeeper leapt away from the customer he'd been serving to bow attentively. Had Victor not been so battered by his last half year in the Netherlands, not to mention his last three days, the offer of assistance would have been welcome.

He looked around, past the harried man with matted curls. It was just a bookshop.

Had he expected to find a new version of himself here? He ought not waste the visit. "Have you any news bills? Leaflets? Anything printed today?"

The man stuttered apologetic denials till Victor feared something in him would burst.

At least he didn't glare like the servants at Hartwick House.

The place should have been emptied of disapproval by his father's death. But no, Victor had missed the last hours of his lordship's deathbed; so even the servants whispered among themselves and hinted with their eyes that he was no kind of suitable heir.

He looked around. This was Allenby's. He knew the place.

The shelves were full of novels, old and new, along with treatises on natural history and philosophy from all corners of the globe. Without intending, he had come to the perfect place to be someone else, living a more pleasant life.

The pretense would last longer if he purchased a book.

"Fine." Victor swept off his hat and surveyed the leather and paper of his surroundings. "What have you for a travel story? Not a diary, something fantastical. I enjoyed *Gulliver's Travels.*"

"Of course, sir." Relieved and recovered, the young man gestured smoothly to a shelf nearby.

"There is a new novel this year that is everything you ask, fantastical and historical at once. It is called *Waverly,* very popular. If that doesn't suit, Mrs. Thomas's *The Prison-House* is selling well, though we don't sell many Minerva Press books to gentlemen." Having proffered the book, he retreated just as quickly, changing his mind at what Victor would like based on his scowl.

Victor wanted to snap his fingers and demand it back. As his father so often pointed out, with his shortcomings, real women were beyond his reach. A fictional woman might at least give him insight into such mysterious creatures.

To his friend in the foreign minister's office, Victor's ability to sit for hours tracing out the details of a contract was invaluable. Women did not find it so.

Unfortunately, it was the best quality he had to offer.

His father's mocking laugh echoed in his mind. Would that death had erased his memories.

With the silent sound ringing in his head, Victor was more curt than he wished to be. "Allow me to study your newer novels myself. I have been abroad."

The messy-haired man waved to the shelf behind which the previous patron he'd been serving had hidden herself, examining each volume closely.

Clearly a woman, the patron had golden curls tumbling out of her bonnet and thick dark lashes laying against cold-flushed cheeks.

Had she seemed real, Victor would not have approached her.

* * *

THE CLOSER HE came to her, the more undeniable it was that she was real. Unaccountably, she made him think of cake.

He was hungry, but he didn't think it was because of his hunger. She was round, and sweet, and looked toothsome. She required nibbling. Like cake.

He became lost in wondering how he knew that.

Food had repelled him for so long that he preferred to forget he had a body. His father had constantly encouraged Victor to take up frequenting whores, swearing it would make Victor a man. But one close look at a lady of the evening, lips painted red, wig pinned to her head, powder applied obviously and copiously to her bosom, had crystallized the matter in Victor's mind. Women hailed from the side of the world that held slick, sticky things like butter sauces and jam. He lived on this side. Alone.

But the woman before him wasn't a butter sauce in a mask; she was real. A person, like him. No matter how delicious others found oysters, or beef stew, or melted cheese, he would never eat such things; yet in her he saw the appeal of something hot and soft against his tongue.

The next moment he shook himself. This was a public place, and he did not purchase women.

Nor was she for sale. Her thick plain clothing spoke of work, like a nurse, perhaps even a housekeeper. It did nothing to draw attention to her curves or soft smile.

She was simply sampling books, taking them up one at a time from a long table and examining their endpapers and first few pages thoroughly, as if for the secrets of ancient mysteries. The golden curls escaping from her dark bonnet stood out on the dark gray of her serviceable coat.

It was her story that interested him most.

She moved to the next heap of volumes.

The shopkeeper, trying to serve all his patrons at once, hopped from place to place all over the shop. A half dozen souls were already milling through the store, with more coming. He occasionally tossed a glare toward the young woman, but she pretended not to see. Or perhaps truly did not.

That cemented Victor's admiration.

His dire need for foreign news forgotten, he picked up a volume on birds that did not interest him at all. It only allowed him to stay in one place, pretending to turn over the plates, peering over drawings of feathers to watch this fascinating creature stalk her pleasure among towers of books.

So of course he noticed when the man approached her.

The interloper was stoutish, and clearly felt the stained linen collar pinned closed around his neck gave him a genteel air. He did not doff his greasy cap.

Victor couldn't hear what the man said. He abandoned the birds and moved to a closer table full of books on cookery. Their printed words before him were a blur; he focused only on hearing.

The man's voice sounded coarse, accustomed to swearing, perhaps shouting. His words were even coarser.

"Come on, love, just round the corner. I'll show you a good time." He moved even closer to the woman's immaculate wool sleeve. Touching it would soil it.

She stood immobile, doubtless from shock.

Victor had never felt part of society, not even part of Britain. Sailing abroad had carried him away from his father's venom, but not his own private struggles. From habit, he looked to the shopkeeper, to see London govern its own.

The shopkeeper stood with two other patrons on the shop's far side, among Roman histories. No help was coming.

Victor pushed habit aside.

"My lady," he called, charging around the shelves to approach with the confidence of someone who knew her well. He had never in his life approached a young lady that way before.

He dropped the book in his hand atop a stack and faced down the ruffian. "I heard what you said."

The man blustered, casting most unwelcome scrutiny over the lady's figure. His chin was a bit crooked, scarred from shaves, or fights, gone wrong. She might be dressed below her station in life, but he was certainly dressed high for his, the once-fine waistcoat soft from wearing, his coat sleeves beginning to fray.

As Victor drew closer, his bluster faded, but he did not go. The more the man leaned closer to the woman beside them, making her lean away, the more Victor's anger swelled, far greater than the burst of temper he'd expended upon a disappointing newspaper.

Victor drew off his glove and slapped it hard across that gross, unshaven face.

The sound of angry leather across skin in the bookshop was shocking. Everything stopped, everyone looked.

Perhaps the months in the Netherlands had done something to him, as for the first time in his life, Victor had no trouble pretending as well as any actor upon the theater boards.

"How dare you speak to my wife?" It might not be pretending. The anger was real.

The ruffian tripped backwards, nearly falling into a table full of books. "I beg yer pardon, sir, I didn't see you with the girl—"

"And what of that?" He turned to the young woman frozen by the table. Truthfully, Victor considered her far more intimidating; he swallowed, but moved closer. If she were his wife, after all, that was what he would do. "You're not harmed?"

She blinked. Her eyes were so large, so bright. In the

dimness of the shop he could not discern their color. "I'm quite well," she said faintly, swaying a little.

The swaying terrified him.

Moving even closer, he braced his hands under her arms. It was unforgivably forward of him, but if she fainted, he could catch her.

She did look like she might faint, her formerly red cheeks bleached white; but she only said, "I didn't understand his question?"

"He can be grateful for that."

Reluctant to touch the man, Victor gave him a glare that felt very natural. "Remove yourself. Be grateful for the lady's mercy, and that I am unarmed, and that blood ruins books."

Turning back to the woman, Victor noted out the corner of his eye that the man stumbled away and out the door. The sweet shop-bell rang again.

He tried to sound just as sweet, saying the first thing that came to his head. "The shop hasn't got any bound copies of *The Lady's Assistant*."

The woman touched a slender finger to the book he'd put down. "But you were holding a copy of *The Lady's Assistant*."

Then she slapped a hand over her own mouth, regarding him with open horror.

Why her own voice upset her, he couldn't guess, but at least her color had come back. Indeed, her cheeks blushed the same rosy, golden color as a summer peach, and again he thought of nibbling.

The shopkeeper chose this moment for his belated arrival.

Victor couldn't tear his eyes away from the woman who still stood there, as wide-eyed as if she were pinned to a sled skewing down a mountainside out of control.

Her alarm moved him to stay as well. He committed to

his actions as fully as he had committed to the action to sail abroad and never see his father again.

Close enough to smell the warm scent of violet soap, a scent that must be coming from her, Victor fought the urge to close his eyes and breathe her in and said, "Your mother will have to wait for us to order it for her."

"My lord, I'm so sorry." That damnable shopkeeper.

Victor's anger had not faded. "For the way you let utter villains accost women in your shop, or for the lack of books ready to sell in a bookshop?"

He let the man sputter while he himself settled into his boots like a man with all the time in the world. He had watched bureaucrats at work, and knew how to convey immovability. To the woman still covering her own mouth beside him, he said, "The printer has unbound copies, and ought to be able to deliver one before twelfth night. Surely that is time enough for a Christmas present? Your mother has never struck me as an impatient woman."

Her mouth only fell open.

Victor had the sense that she was about to say something that would give the lie to his little play.

"Excuse us," he told the sweating shopkeeper. "I must speak to my wife alone."

And shifting his grip to just one of her elbows, which was far too little, he ushered her out the door, making the shop bell tinkle one more time.

* * *

Isabel was horrified with herself.

All her parents' warning lectures had come true in the space of minutes. She had traveled unaccompanied; it had gotten her unwanted attention. She'd been accosted; she'd frozen, not knowing what to do or say. And worst of all, when a gentleman—*a real gentleman,* as was obvious from his gold watch-chain and the fur of his hat—had rescued her, she had corrected him like he was a schoolboy.

This walking nightmare was of her own making.

Now he ushered her out of the shop, quietly asking, "Are you quite well?"

"No!" It felt like a shout but sounded like a whisper. "I am frightened and ashamed. I still have no book. And you've never met my mother."

Even now she said everything she shouldn't. This was why Mr. Ball and Mr. Wheelock had married distant friends, not her.

She tried to curtsey. His arm came under hers again, not letting her. It was warm and shockingly strong.

"What are you doing?" he hissed.

"What are *you* doing? I mean, my lord—" She tried to curtsey again, making him work to keep her upright; they engaged in a silent, invisible struggle. "I am sure I should call you my lord *something.*"

The gentleman before her winced. His deep-set eyes kept peering at her, alarming her, then the softness of his lips let her breathe. A muscle flexed in his square-set jaw as he glanced after the greasy departed man, and the cycle began all over again.

"Sadly, I do not know your mother," he said, keeping his voice quiet. "It was all I could think of to say."

"I'm so sorry. I am *so* sorry. It's only that you were *holding* a copy of *The Lady's Assistant.*"

He brushed away the idea of books. "The gentleman was accosting you."

"Yes." Isabel looked over her shoulder. He was gone. The itching crawling along her spine had not gone away. "I'm so sorry."

The gentleman slid his other hand under her forearm too.

As before, it both steadied her and made her want to rear back. He was such a dark glower of a man.

His lips weren't frightening. Slowly Isabel tried to breathe and only see the softness there.

He murmured, "You did nothing wrong."

Had she not? She still had only the haziest idea what the man intended. She had just been immobilized by the shock of it, by the need to parse what he was saying very carefully. Somehow even by holding still she had done something wrong. It had been nothing like sitting with Mr. Ball or Mr. Wheelock in a parlor while her mother knitted by the fire. She couldn't tell if masculine attention was supposed to come in a form like this. "I came out of doors." She couldn't explain herself; the words just tumbled out.

Confusion flickered through his shadowed eyes. Isabel hated herself.

"And now," she said on an indrawn breath, "now you will think I am simple atop everything else, and I am not, I don't think I am, it is only that my maid went home for Christmas and I thought it would be an adventure to buy a book but—" She caught at the words running away like an untethered horse, yanked herself back from the brink, then added with obvious reluctance, "I'm not supposed to have adventures, am I?"

His confusion flickered and went out like a flame leaving him stony. "Madame, *you* did *nothing wrong*."

"How should I *know?*" The last she nearly hissed at him. "I have spent my life in a drawing room waiting for some man to notice me, and that one did."

It was more than she'd ever planned to say to anyone. About her sad lack of prospects, about her dull life, about any of it. Yet it had just come tumbling out after the other words. Words were betraying her.

She'd never had this much trouble being quiet with any man before.

His hands felt big, huge in fact, and Isabel thought it odd that she mostly noticed when they dropped away. The cold air soothed her hot cheeks.

And the gentleman before her began to lecture.

There was no other word for what he did. He settled into his own words and brooked no interruption.

"Madame. It may be that you have resided in a county of fools and no man has taken it upon himself to visit or court you appropriately. And now for whatever reason you find yourself alone in the city, in straitened circumstances." His eyes wandered over her coat. "Nonetheless, I assure you the attention you were just paid is not the sort a lady deserves. I cannot believe I have to explain this."

Isabel's nerves had already been tightly wound by walking through the city alone through so many people. She had trembled with agitation when the man had accosted her, her training toward silence warring with her instinct to scream.

The terror of it was so deep that it made her angry, and that helped hold her tears back.

"I am not an idiot," she told him clearly, glad they had come outside. She stayed quiet enough that the passers-by would not necessarily hear; but she was angry enough not to care if they did. "In fact, I can read. That is why I am *shopping*. At a *bookseller's*. My circumstances are not *straitened;* this is a very serviceable coat. And the men of my county are not fools—"

Suddenly she heard what she was saying and drew in a quick breath.

She'd never said it aloud. The men were not fools. She was simply no prize.

Blinking fast enough to keep back the tears, the flooding

sudden realization that there was nothing wrong with the men in her neighborhood, that her parents were right, that it was *her*, it all made Isabel press a hand to her waist inside her muff, hoping he would not notice.

She managed to say, "And you also addressed me very familiarly."

"I didn't offer to ravish you in an alley."

The word *ravish* did something horrible to Isabel's insides. Her terror tripled. "You dragged me outside!"

His exasperated huff drew her attention back to his face, and she realized he had never stopped looking at her.

"You are right. My deepest apologies. I have spent too much time in the company of men, and only abrupt ones. And too much time lecturing. If you wish to shop, then let me accompany you."

That simple offer made Isabel's heart pound harder than the crude words of the man who had just accosted her.

This man had a regal tilt to his head and tall hat. The clothes he wore were clearly not his only ones. His very bearing screamed *quality*. And he was offering to shop with her because he wished her to be safe.

"No." What was wrong with her mouth today? She'd just let a common rogue say things to her no lady should hear; now this gentleman offered to accompany her shopping and she rebuffed him. Perhaps she *had* caught a fever walking out of doors.

And the gentleman just peered at her with those deep-set eyes. "Truly?" he snapped as if he could not believe what he was hearing either.

"No." Isabel's knees almost buckled with the relief of the opportunity to take back her stupid words, think them through again, say something different. "I mean, no, I do not truly mean it."

If she were going to speak, she must do better at it.

"Please." She did not like beginning that way. She pretended she hadn't said it. "Sir. Of course I don't wish to be attacked. He spoke quietly to me; you spoke quietly to me. He was unwashed while you are clean, though both of you show a lack of recent shaving. You are clearly wealthier; is that how I should know this conversation is safe?"

"*NO.*" Catching himself, he reined in his temper. He seemed prone to bursts of that. Isabel was not frightened of *that,* but it was precisely her lack of self-preservation they were discussing.

Making another dissatisfied, irritated noise, he reached a hand toward her again; then stopped and pulled it back. Isabel only watched with interest.

"No." This time he said it more calmly, one wide gloved hand upright like a stone street-marker between them. "Plenty of wealthy men are worse villains than the one we sent away." His already deep eyes narrowed. "But you know that."

"I don't."

"You do." He pointed at the street. Isabel turned to look at the people walking by, rolling by in open barouches despite the chill weather, or atop wagons of barrels and bales for sale. He pointed at a passing man, one who gave him a look that said *I beg your pardon?* and kept walking. "Does that man make you recoil? Like a snake you found under a rock?" His voice was pitched to reach only her ears.

"I'm not frightened of snakes. But no."

"There is your instinct. Snakes do not set out to harm you. Nor do some men. But many do, and you must heed your instinct."

Isabel studied him closely. His fine voice sounded note-like as it rose and fell, as clear as plucked strings on a harpsichord. *No,* she decided, *more like the vibrating notes of an organ that at a moment's warning could sink very low.*

"You're an intimidating man," she said, voice quivering but determined even in the face of his storm-cloud eyes and bristled bones. "You are lecturing me on my own instincts. Should I trust someone like you?"

He winced, and Isabel jumped backwards, horrified again at the things she said.

He pulled her closer again, so much heat radiating from him she could feel it even through her coat.

"No," he said through teeth gritted so hard she could see the muscle clench in his jaw. "I rescind everything I said. You were right, I was wrong. There is no way to tell who I am from a glance, or what I might do in five minutes or five years. Avoid everyone like me." He consulted the gold watch from his watch-pocket, slid it back. "But I am here now, and might never have been of use to anyone before, so you might as well make use of me now. If you wish to shop, let me accompany you."

His words were sad, but Isabel felt an odd thrill at the way he spoke of her making use of him. "Are you doing a kind deed for Christmas? Accompanying a stranger?"

"I called you my wife. Call me anything you like."

Her spirits tumbled. It was hard to know *how much* of an adventure she was having.

He clearly had no intention of giving his name, but he had not corrected her *my lord.* By rights he should not be speaking to her; he should not even *see* her. But he had; he'd seen her accosted and righted it.

Across the street, above the shops, inside someone's merry apartment already lit with candles and full of laughing people, Isabel could see a ball of mistletoe, white berries flashing in the deep greenery like surprises. "Very well, Lord Mistletoe. I believe I do trust you."

The muscle jumped again. "You shouldn't," was all he said

before his hand rose again under her elbow and he ushered her back inside.

The shop was the same, warmer than out of doors but dark, and the shop-bell tinkled overhead.

But the bookseller's attitude was very different. He abandoned his other patrons with break-neck speed. "Sir. Since you and your wife both asked for novels, I took the liberty of placing a selection over there." He gestured to a small table against the far wall, out of the swirl of other patrons. "I hope you will be comfortable. Allenby's is very grateful for your custom."

Isabel's heart pounded again.

It might be a bit dim for perusing printed pages, but it was quite companionable for two.

For this gentleman. And his *wife*.

Her Lord Mistletoe seemed quite comfortable with this ruse and accepted the premise that of course they wished to shop together. "Excellent," was all he said before escorting her to the table in the corner.

She knew her hand was still trembling. The work of her nerves this past hour! She steadied it by picking up the top book. "*Gulliver's Travels,*" she read from its spine.

"Foolish. I told him I've read it; why would I want to buy it again?" The gentleman's impatience was palpable, yet he only said, "What else has he given us?"

Us. There was a word no one had ever applied to her before.

It steadied her. She picked up the next book with surer hands, as if she were indeed a wife—she, *a wife*—helping her husband choose something to read for his entertainment. "This one is Mrs. Burney's latest, but you won't want that."

"Why not?" His question was as keen and clear as the sound of his voice. He sincerely wanted to know why this book might not serve.

"It is called *The Wanderer, or Female Difficulties.*" Isabel didn't explain why she doubted that a man would want to read it.

"I find myself very curious about female difficulties." He expressed no mockery, only sharp interest. "What do you think of the first page?"

Unlike her previous accoster, this gentleman's attention was on all of her. Not just her body, which had never been of interest to anyone before, but her eyes on the page, her mind reading the words. The things she said.

The previous man, the first who had ever spoken to her without introduction, was like the thick green sludge at the edges of ponds, sticky and repulsive.

This man was like a wave from the sea threatening to topple her over.

As new experiences went, it was overwhelming. Beyond any adventure she could have expected traveling alone on Christmas Eve.

Amid her jangled nerves, pounding heart, and flushed skin, she realized she was enjoying it.

Adventures have ups and downs to them, she realized. No wonder she had always been warned away from them.

Isabel turned all the pages of the book's long dedication. The author apparently had a great deal to say to her husband in print.

When the Roman numerals disappeared, she drew the book closer to her eyes. "Quite a thrilling story, I expect."

"What makes you say so?" He had no subterfuge to the question, no sly innuendo. He wanted to know why she thought what she thought. Of a book.

"It opens during the Terror. In the dark and damp of December." She smiled at him, eyes lifting from the page, and his serious expression was still fixed on hers. The parallel of the moment, their own damp December though the sun had not yet set, connected the two of them then, and their eyes showed they both recognized the connection between them and the novel. "It is English passengers in a boat preparing to embark for Britain, I suppose, when a French voice cries out for pity."

"Man or woman?"

"Are we to guess from the title? No, it does say." Isabel turned the page, skipping words to pick out the answer to his question. "A woman. Cries of agony, it says!"

"Cries of agony? That sounds frightful. I suppose a novelist must have grist for her mill. What say you, my lady, is it worth reading on?"

CHAPTER 3

The way she jumped when he called her *my lady* only made Victor want to do it again. Not to pain her, but to accustom her. She seemed starved for recognition of any sort, and Victor wanted to repair that. There was only so much one could do in a bookshop.

Not that he should say or do anything. Everything pouring out of him this afternoon reminded him of the inheritance of his father. Not the title or the estate, but his callous treatment of women, his frightening aspect, his constant lack of sympathy.

Victor had ventured to the Americas to find sympathy. He'd wanted to see the plight of kidnapped sailors first-hand. He'd studied the law to understand sympathy. Gone to Ghent because of it, he'd thought.

Yet in the end he was his father's only legally-begotten child, and apparently had inherited something of his personality as well as his goods.

It was a revolting thought.

At least here in this bookshop, the sun had set, candles were lit, and a small but steady trickle of customers assuaged

Victor's guilt that for all intents and purposes, he and this unknown woman were treating it like their own private library.

She was a feast for all the senses Victor feared to indulge. Her smile was soft, quick to come but also to go; her voice was low, a little thick, reminding him of honey. The curves that showed under her coat when she reached across the table to pick up a far volume made his body tense, made him feel like a wolf preparing to spring. When she laughed it was worse.

Why was she not married? Why was such a toothsome morsel of a woman shopping alone at all, much less on Christmas Eve? Had she no mother or father to take care of her? No home of her own?

Britain was a land of fools. Fools like his father, shooting, drinking, and purchasing whores. Victor should go back to the Americas. He should go back to Ghent.

He should have finished his work instead of listening to others and coming home.

"It's purely unnatural to have no interest in women." His father had said so time after time. His hectoring had pushed Victor to pretend even less interest than he had. By the time he'd survived sixteen years of relentless fault-finding, Victor's only pleasure was thwarting his father's every expectation.

He'd rather have absorbed any number of filthy insults— and did—about his supposed proclivities for men, or boys, or perhaps sheep, before giving his father the satisfaction of knowing that they shared even one taste.

As he also could not abide society's extraordinarily dull affairs of drinking and dancing in stuffy ballrooms with too many people and nothing he wished to eat, he'd also had few chances to meet women suitable for more than an evening's liaison.

And regarding the ones available for evening liaisons, he had even less patience.

He truly tried to have sympathy for everyone his father didn't. That included prostitutes. But their lack of real interest in him, the blank cupidity of their eyes as they estimated not him but the weight of his purse, turned his stomach more surely than the thick sauces served on all the food.

Victor kept alive on apples, bread, and turnips, and the company of his own right hand.

Now he was starving in a London bookshop.

Starving for food as always, but also for *company*. This woman, whoever she was, had a fleet and agile intellect, and no shortage of words. And she was not *dull*.

Why hadn't he properly introduced himself?

She looked up at him, eyes sparkling in the bright tallow-candle light. "I don't wish to appear scandalous, but the words *moral* and *decent* don't speak to me of a particularly engaging novel."

What on earth did she mean?

Oh, the book.

She was so delightfully prim and so determined to ignore propriety at the same time.

He felt himself almost smile. "You prefer your novels more wicked, madame?"

The peach-pink flush that flooded her cheeks when he shocked her was delicious. Hungry, indeed.

She should *not* consider him trustworthy.

And indeed she did give him a disapproving look. "I do not ask my novels to be *wicked*. I merely want something beyond moralization."

He raised his head. "Perhaps we should investigate other offerings beyond the novels."

"A splendid idea!" She lit up like one of the candles. There was no sarcasm to her, and no cynicism, which only made Victor wonder more how she had come to be in London alone.

The shelves in the middle of the room must be stacked in some order, but Victor did not know it. Apparently, neither did his companion; she apparently stepped to the nearest one from an enthusiasm born of curiosity.

"*The Natural History Of Quadrupeds and Cretaceous Animals.* My goodness. Did I pronounce that right? Oh! A tiger!" The volume fell open in her hands at its most popular plate, and she jumped a little at the appearance of the orange-striped beast.

It made him draw close behind her. "I have no idea if your pronunciation is correct, but it sounded fine to me." He studied the image over her shoulder. Victor caught a wisp of the scent of her, warmth and candle smoke and the soap she must have used to wash herself.

It was impossible to keep his thoughts from turning animal.

"Do you care for animals?" She turned and her face was so close to his. The question, so near his brutish thoughts, wrenched him out of them. "I should know that already, should I not?" she asked more softly. He wondered if she meant because she maintained she was no fool, or because they were pretending to be married.

They stood so close.

No closer than reasonable for a wife and husband in public. Perhaps if newly wed.

Still closer than any other woman had ever been. And more pleasurable.

"I have no great fondness for animals," Victor admitted under his breath, continuing their game, sorry to disappoint her. "Perhaps I should visit more farms."

She gave him one of her fleeting, sincerely sweet smiles.

"Only if you find a farm to feed you. You are too thin." Before Victor could grow self-conscious—he *was*, and he knew it— she moved on and resumed her game, delivering a wifely line aloud as she put down the book. "I don't believe natural history was ever your taste."

It was a relief, like a heavy weight from his chest. She saw how he was and neither ignored nor belittled him. She had not descended into a catalog of his faults, only observed and moved on.

If the game was to be someone he was not, he couldn't. He answered truthfully. "No. The law has always been my only interest. But I wish to improve myself." He meant it.

* * *

Isabel had a dozen questions. He must be a solicitor—or a barrister! They had always seemed so important. Did he send letters to magistrates? To Parliament? To the Regent himself?

He seemed like someone she would trust if she were charged with a crime. Upright. Serious. But humane. There were flashes of humor behind his wooden façade. There was a person inside there.

He advised her not to trust him, but she found it impossible not to be curious.

Did lords have trades? She didn't know. The lord of their county was a baron, round as an egg and just as fragile; he kept a steady stream of physicians visiting his house, but had no trade.

This game required her to keep searching for a book for her false husband when she would rather drop all pretense and interrogate him in the middle of a bookstore.

"I hardly think you need improvement." She could say that in all truth. He was too thin, and a bit serious; there were hollows behind his jutting jaw and at his wrists, and his clothes were loose. But he was wonderfully attentive, his quick questions and answers full of insight into the books and, uncomfortably, her.

It had never occurred to Isabel that she could simply be what she was, a country spinster living out her years in a rented room alone, and still have an interesting conversation.

Perhaps *this* was the freedom of being unwanted.

It certainly bolstered her as she moved on through the shelves trying to guess his tastes. "You picked up the *Lady's Assistant*, but surely you don't want any books of cookery?"

"No," he said with an odd grimace.

She didn't press.

Her fingers ran down the spines of the next shelves. "Would you care for a play? Or poetry?" The slim volume she removed opened to its first page of text.

She read quietly,

Still must I hear?—shall hoarse Fitzgerald bawl
His creaking couplets in a tavern hall,
And I not sing, lest, haply, Scotch Reviews
Should dub me scribbler, and denounce my Muse?
Prepare for rhyme—I'll publish, right or wrong:
Fools are my theme, let Satire be my song.

"I don't understand," said Isabel as she looked up. The gentleman stood right at her elbow. "Apparently we've come in at the middle of a conversation." That *we* felt as comfortable as wool slippers and as exciting as fireworks.

His expression was that of a man carefully considering. "Apparently Scotch Reviews has upset the gentleman. *Scribbler* is surely an insult."

"So he'll publish, right or wrong? Imagine writing a whole book as a tantrum!" Isabel closed the book. "Purchasing it would only indulge him."

Then she looked up, openly apologetic.

"I'm sorry, I didn't mean to speak for you—"

"Why apologize when your opinion is the right one?"

His words turned all Isabel's bones to marbles, rolling over each other and racing for the floor. She braced a hand against the table to stay upright.

How many times had she apologized for being right? Dozens. Hundreds. *Millions.*

Being right was her least attractive quality. Her mother had always said so. "A man doesn't want correction, Isabel. Do restrain yourself."

She'd restrained herself as best she could, and all it had gotten her was a lonely room in Leicester Square.

Perhaps she should forget about restraint.

* * *

VICTOR DIDN'T WANT to play this game any more.

It limited her conversation to books. "Look how cleverly this map of Africa unfolds!" She bent close to the pages. "The land of Bournou. The great desert of Zaara. I believe I would rather have a traveler's diary than a map, but the names are so alluring. Wergela. Gadamis. Cairo."

He wanted to ask her about *her.* Everything he didn't know. He'd like a diary of every day of her life from birth.

Attention to detail had saved his life, given him a purpose; it was a useful skill even barristers often did not have. It was his only tool, his only weapon.

It had gained him a place at the table of diplomacy, a place where he watched every face, read every proposed word of the treaty in progress, advising the delegation how the meaning changed with each new paragraph or even comma.

It was his life, and he had never been able to discuss it with anyone. He wanted to now.

But the young woman seemed to enjoy skipping from

book to book, not the least inclined to share any personal details.

If she wished to play this game he would, but he was finding it more and more painful.

They paused among volumes of geography.

And she did share something. "I have always wanted to go abroad," she confided, running her fingers over the books' spines.

He wanted to kiss those fingertips.

He'd never had such a thought before. He kept it, as he kept all his thoughts, to himself.

But the sudden onrushing desire, something he'd never felt before, made him bold.

Reaching over her shoulder, he plucked out a bound collection of Welsh maps. "I thought next summer we should visit the Welsh north. See the mountains. Take long walks."

This time when she looked up at him he held her gaze.

What could she see in his eyes? How he truly longed to do exactly that? How he imagined checking his stride so it would match hers?

Or did she only see his sad lack of experience with women? The weakness in him his father always derided?

His desperate loneliness?

Her eyes held neither shock nor pity; they looked far away, dreaming, perhaps of walks in Wales. "Wouldn't that be lovely?" she whispered.

He wanted to whisper back. *Yes.*

"Has your wife found any books that please you?" asked the bookseller, pausing as he passed with more books in his arms.

Victor felt the lady stiffen, realized they were so close their bodies brushed.

His quiet mother had lived a stifled life and died when he was a boy. At the other end of the spectrum of his father's women, whores out for coin were generally brash, desperate. He had no idea what a woman would be like if she were cherished.

Perhaps something like this.

There was no gentle way of discussing any of this with her. Instead he just asked her, "Mrs. Burney's book appealed to you most, did it not?" He eyed that book in its flat leather binding; it still lay on their corner table. He would forever think of that spot as *theirs*. Atop it were two other novels. "You wanted those three, if I recall. Bound in leather."

The shop would bind and deliver whatever they picked. He had a vision of her reclining on a chaise, one of these books in her soft hands, its pebbled leather under her fingertips. He felt himself harden.

"Oh no, no no," she shook her head quickly, and Victor noticed that she'd paled. It chilled him like spray on the winter sea.

The shopkeeper's cheeriness drooped, but soldiered on. "But you would still like them, sir?"

Victor swept a glance over the table. He'd take them all, if only to remind him of this evening.

His habit was never to move or speak quickly. He'd cultivated it to set him further apart from his father. It remained valuable in both travel and law. Now it saved him from giving in to his most vehement urge, which was to sweep all these books to the floor, set this woman upon this table, and rip apart the plain wool she wore until—

Shaken, he took a deeper breath. "We have not yet made any decisions."

The *we* was for the game. To steady her. But as the shopkeeper departed, her eyes remained wide with alarm.

That he could not stand. "What has frightened you?"

"Not frightened, but—you must think me so—terribly

common," she stammered, dropping her eyes. "To meet in these circumstances, accosted by that man—"

"His fault, not yours," Victor said calmly, trying to press down on everything roiling in him.

"—I *chide* you, then spend *hours* talking to you *so* familiarly, of course you think me a—of course you think I expect to be paid, but I am not—"

Understanding dawned. "You think *I* believe you want to be paid in *books?*"

She leaned closer to whisper, which was delightful. Under her breath she said, "I am not a... I do not..."

"Let me set your mind at ease," he said just as quietly. "I do not think you prostitute yourself for books."

"Oh." The flush on her cheeks was blazing now. She was too impossibly innocent to be wandering London by herself, his—

"I would like to know your name." The words were out before he could stop them, before he could consider how they broke the rules of their little game.

"Oh," she said again. She put her hands on her cheeks as if to hide the fire in them. "But that's not—it isn't a more gentle way of asking me into the alley?"

Victor did not blush. He never had reason.

Now he felt warmth in his face.

"No," he simply said, though the image of ravishing her in an alley was in every way appealing. Had he more idea how it was done, he might even suggest it. At least he differed from his father in feeling the urge only around a woman not suited for it. "You are kind and I only wish to know the name of the lady providing such delightful company."

"I feel more lucky than kind."

His heart leaped at the idea that she was enjoying this, enjoying *him.*

Still she kept her eyes down, and her voice still trembled

as she added softly, "This is foolish, but I simply must trust your answer to this question. Is this a sort of... a sort of accosting that proceeds more politely?"

Victor wanted to laugh. He didn't, because she would think he was laughing at her. But he felt his cheeks pulling toward an unusual new position. Smiling. He could only tell her the truth. "The answer to that is not simple. I encourage you not to trust me."

She knew, somehow she suspected. The urge he had. Urges. The ones he was suppressing.

If she did suspect, she didn't say so. She said, "I only came for a new book for myself. Something exciting to while away my Christmas days, and now—"

"Yes?" he prompted her to go on.

"Now my afternoon has been more exciting than any book. Perhaps I don't need one after all."

CHAPTER 4

*I*sabel found it intoxicating to be liked. Only a few hours in this gentleman's company and he appeared to like her far better than Mr. Ball or Mr. Wheelock ever had.

And the things she found herself saying. They were only true; but truth had never served her in the past. She couldn't believe how well it was going now.

The gentleman beside her greeted this news as he did everything, with serious concentration. Isabel wondered what it would be like to have that concentration centered longer upon her.

My.

He noticed her shiver.

"The hour is late and the shop grows chilled," he said in that way that she liked, simple, direct. "Don't let me disrupt your plans."

Disrupt her plans? He'd disrupted her *dreams.* She had always thought of Mr. Ball and Mr. Wheelock as charges. Responsibilities. She'd have watched over their houses and meals, and if she were lucky, their children. The details of how that would happen were murky, but she knew it involved getting close. That part she had tried not to imagine.

Now she could imagine nothing else.

She knew nothing of Lord Mistletoe's house or meals, or how to keep them. Nor did she wish to learn.

She wanted to know what the skin of his throat was like there where it disappeared under his neckcloth. Wanted to tuck a scarf around his neck when he went out into the chill.

Wanted him to stay in with her, and keep her warm.

Wanted him to explain the law, or walks in Wales, anything, absolutely anything he wished to say to her.

He looked sad as his blunt gloved fingers settled upon the little stack of novels. "Not that I know your plans. Just... do as you intended, and so shall I."

"What do you intend?" The question slipped out before she could hold it back.

"To return to the Continent."

"Oh." The disappointment was physical. Cold and sickening in her stomach. "To live?"

"I had a life there. A kind of life." There flashed some of the irritation, the bitterness, he'd worn when he'd walked in the door. Only hours ago, but it felt like a distant memory returned.

Isabel did not want to contradict, only gently question. "But if you don't enjoy it?"

"The solitude of being an unwelcome foreigner is preferable to the solitude of being unwelcome at home."

His honesty called for hers. "I think so too."

His eyes flashed as they met her gaze, then dropped.

She hoped she hadn't offended. He'd put words to something she'd felt, that was all. London was very different from anything she'd known, but she preferred her lonely room here to a place among disappointed family.

His taciturn bitterness should have driven her away. She did not really know him. Perhaps this was his true self. Angry, hard.

But she didn't think so.

She felt balanced on a string over a deep, deep chasm. She had tried so hard to please her former suitors, and they had chosen elsewhere. Now this gentleman seemed well-disposed toward her for doing nothing. Isabel could not imagine why she interested him. She could not imagine it would persist.

She was trying hard to think of something clever that would amuse him, soften him, let her find out why he was so troubled today, let her plumb more of his history.

But before she could think what to say, the bookseller returned.

And her erstwhile rescuer made another decision for her. "The lady will have these," he spread his hand over the little group of novels, "and anything else she likes." He looked around as if just realizing where he was. "I believe you have an account for my family. Lord Hartwick."

He *was* a lord!

Isabel swallowed. Here she was, spinning fantasies of little cottages in Wales, and he was a *lord*. Not only had she never met anyone titled, her *family* had never met anyone titled. They had only seen the local baron when he drove by in his carriage.

Her father's earnings had a sheen of gentility as long as they stayed in the country. In the city, his name was connected only to the scent of beer. He owned pubs and breweries and his descendants would not inherit a title. Ever.

No wonder the gentleman thought her common. Compared to him, she was.

Finally Isabel stopped swirling over what she had already suspected and faced the worse truth. He was not any fanciful

Lord Mistletoe; he was Lord Hartwick, and he spoke of his *family.*

There must already be a Lady Hartwick. No wonder he kept her at arm's length. He conversed so easily with her from experience, because he was married.

Here she had interpreted his attention as—well, as flirtation. She was the most appalling fool. This was the most appalling afternoon.

The most pleasant one of her life, yet she must hurry home to die of embarrassment in private.

Whatever had kept him here, he now moved quickly to depart. The swing of his greatcoat followed him through the little room. He seemed to survey it all from a height, and find none of it particularly pleasing. "Whatever the lady wants. She will give you the direction. Good afternoon."

Then with the most haunting look, he turned to her. "Good afternoon, madame."

Isabel could not imagine a man giving such a good-bye to his wife.

So longing. So sad.

If her Lord Mistletoe *was* married, then something was terribly wrong.

Abruptly he'd gone, yet their words felt so unfinished that Isabel was compelled to follow him into the street. She stood, open-mouthed with surprise, upon the pavement as he waved to a hackney carriage.

Immediately it rolled their way.

Apparently the gentleman regretted giving his name. No doubt he feared blackmail. He worked for the law; importuning young women in bookstores could not be attached to his reputation. Isabel had a faint idea it was illegal as well as immoral.

"Whoa there." The carriage's fat, red-faced driver snapped

his reins; its horse danced to a stop, making its wheels rock. It seemed too small for the man beside her.

His greatcoat flapped as he swept up to it, a black eagle in rain-spattered wool.

She had to say something before he disappeared. She would never see him again. "I apologize for my silly game." It was all she could say without blurting out too much truth in the street. A plain, plumpish country girl could not have hurt such a man; yet he looked hurt, and she wanted to reassure him without saying aloud *I would never cause you pain.*

He looked down at her from the little carriage's window. Unreadable. Stiff. Nothing like the last few hours. "Games, madame, have winners and losers. Has either of us won?"

Frozen in place by the chill of his words, she watched the driver lift his reins. She was confused, spinning, convinced she would never see him again, that she would forever regret this moment.

She rushed forward. "I don't—"

"Madame!" He was so fast. He'd opened the door and shouted in the instant she stepped towards him; she let her impulse carry her forward, into the waiting door. She didn't remember the rest of what she was going to say.

He touched her again, this time his wide hands under both her arms. He hauled her closer, her knees steadying on the floor of the carriage. His deep-set eyes were wide with something like fright. "The wheels could crush you."

She knelt, uncaring of her clothes, one hand in its thin wool mitten balanced on the seat beside him. "Everything will be fine once we've parted," she gasped, hardly knowing what she meant.

"Of course." Still simple, decisive. "Yet the parting is agony."

Before she deciphered his words, his hands, still around

her, grasped her, pulled her towards him, as if she weighed nothing.

His stony face crumbled into a mix of despair, hunger, longing, an agony she'd never seen before and hoped never to see again.

And he kissed her.

It was so quick, and yet time slowed and Isabel registered each impression like a separate bolt of lightning to her core. The length of his eyelashes against his cheek as his eyes closed. The shocking softness of his lips. His skin against hers, his face aligned to hers, sliding close, sliding away.

It was over far too quickly, the most incredible flood of sensations barely touching her then gone, leaving her with the taste of him as he set her—impossibly strong—back on her knees. For an instant she hoped he would drive away with her still kneeling on the carriage floor.

Instead his hands moved her backwards and he barked sharply at the driver to keep the horses still.

She found herself on her feet again, cold hard paving stones underneath.

"Now be careful," he said solemnly before he closed the door again, and Isabel just glimpsed the hackney driver above looking down with a red-cheeked wink.

Then the carriage rolled into the street, soon hidden by wagons and horses and other people walking. In moments it was soon gone.

Isabel drifted back into the store. She felt like she was already waiting for him to return.

He couldn't simply be *gone.* Not so quickly. Not finally. Surely.

She imagined herself climbing up to sit beside him on his carriage seat. Or staying at his feet. Why had she let him go? He was the only thing that had ever happened to her.

The only thing that had not hurt, she corrected herself.

She drifted among the bookshop's tables. The books, so absorbing an hour before, now seemed pointless.

Why had she not asked his direction?

Why had she not given him her name?

"Ah, Lady Hartwick." The always-inconvenient bookseller bustled after her, coat bristling with pleasure at the impending sale. "Your husband mentioned these three novels, and... were there other items you wished to purchase?"

"I'd like to sit." Her legs weren't working.

Had she just knelt between his knees? *Had that been real?*

Most solicitously, the bookseller, less sweaty now that night had fallen, escorted her back to their table, dashed away and came back in seconds with a stool. He bowed and offered it, his wool coat creaking.

Isabel just numbly sat.

What had just happened to her? Hours of living in a dream. One where she belonged to someone. One with possibilities.

She would never visit Cairo or even Wales; it had been pleasant to imagine such things with someone else. Someone who wasn't constantly correcting her speech, her looks, or both.

Then the horrifying reality of the gulf between them, and that she had been spinning pleasant fantasies about someone else's husband.

All capped with the chill of his departure, which had been shattered by the heat of his hands, his pull, his sudden kiss.

She had no idea what had happened. She certainly had no idea what she should do next.

It was impossible to take the books he had offered her.

She had failed him somehow. She had so enjoyed the last few hours, then in an instant he was gone, in more distress than he'd arrived. Somehow she had failed to make their game as much fun for him as it had been for her.

Then a temper she didn't know she had reared its head. He'd enjoyed their time together, and should not have. No wonder he said not to trust him. If he were married...

Rather, he *was* married, and ought not to let another woman pretend to be his wife.

Not even for shopping.

Certainly not for that *kiss*.

Isabel was a staid, quiet person. It was not her nature to have all these whirling impulses fighting inside her, all these impulses to soothe him, berate him, and kiss him all at once.

And feed him. She definitely wanted to feed him. He was far too thin.

His wife could not be taking proper care of him. Perhaps she did not love him. Perhaps she hated him. Perhaps that was why he intended to live on the Continent.

Perhaps he was *ill.*

Spreading a hand on the table's top, Isabel used it to steady herself. She was too sturdy to faint. Her mother had often said so. Now she felt the danger of it looming, another thing she'd never imagined that today had threatened her twice.

Was he ill? Was that why he had looked so sad, so hopeless? Was he *seriously* ill? His wife might be taking the best care of him she could.

Or perhaps she wasn't, and that was even worse.

Night had fallen. It was Christmas Eve. Shouts and cries of laughter sounded faintly outside the gray paned windows. Isabel was alone.

And the gentleman had left her with nothing but the power to purchase books.

She had to think. There must be something she could do. Unless she intended to spend the rest of her life on this stool, she must decide *something,* and she could not think what with her mind spinning like this.

She picked up another volume and stared at it without seeing, willing her mind to settle and to think.

* * *

THE BOOKSELLER, increasingly desperate for his sale after all these hours, brought her volume after volume.

Slowly her thoughts settled. Outside, merchants lit oil lamps along the street, and in their dancing yellow light her thoughts settled into forms she could comprehend.

Of course her first thought was what she had done wrong. That was always how her mother had started every conversation. What she had said, eaten, stitched, or worn incorrectly.

Today those were mere distractions.

Outside the cross-paned windows she saw women walking by, woolen shawls pulled over their heads against the cold. Many of them walked alone. London was full of women who were not fine ladies.

Nor was Isabel a fine lady.

In this evening's orange light she could see that her father's money had bought her some of the trappings of a lady but none of the substance. She could read, do sums, draw ivy vines. She could pluck out tunes on the harpsichord. But she had no real skills, no tutors. The nurse she'd shared with her sister had instructed her a little, then Isabel had done her best.

Which was never very good, according to her mother.

What must his Lady Hartwick be like? Gowned in silk, Isabel had no doubt, with hair dressed in the most fashionable Grecian curls. She must have a tiny waist and a refined bosom that looked good in Continental fashions. She probably spoke French and Italian and drew the most elegant flowers. Perhaps flowers she'd seen on walks in Wales. Or even abroad.

Such an accomplished woman must know many ways to please him. The *him* that loomed large now in her mind. It was simply impossible to think of him as Lord Hartwick. Her Lord Mistletoe, she *knew*. Knew something of his tastes, his wit, his passion.

Lord Mistletoe was innocent. He'd come to this shop with no intention of making her acquaintance and left it with no hint that their acquaintance would continue.

He'd done nothing more improper than speak to her in a familiar way.

Except that kiss.

He had not looked happy because he was *not* happy. The possibility was in him.

Isabel knew that, as surely as she knew her father was happy when not at home. She'd seen it in him when he returned, smelling of beer and friendly fireplaces. She saw it fall away when he crossed their threshold. She'd never realized it before now, but she knew the look of a man unhappy at home.

Her Lord Mistletoe did not have to be taciturn; she knew it the same way she knew he ought not to be so thin. The way she knew he had a fine mind and was generous and kind. Their time together had been brief, but she'd learned so much.

Especially about herself.

She'd left her room near Leicester Square with every intention of purchasing a book and returning home to live out her Christmas, her year, her life in those same dull walls.

One conversation with a stranger—no, two, she reminded herself of her first accoster with a wince of shame—and Isabel had learned she was too curious for that.

She wanted things not found within those walls. She wanted company. She wanted conversation. She wanted to learn more things, and she wanted to do more than wait to die.

She wanted more kisses.

Pressing a hand to her cheek so its warmth wouldn't show, she turned a page of the book in front of her without knowing what it was.

An idea bloomed in her that had never crossed her mind before in any way.

A shocking, terrible, fantastic, horrible idea.

She might never be a wife. She certainly would not be a lady. Nor did she wish to be a prostitute, not for books or any other purchasable pleasures.

But what if she were a mistress?

The belonging, the *tie* to such a man was out of reach. But what if the man was not?

She could imagine him coming to her little room, where she might boil him fresh eggs. There was an excellent bakery nearby where she could buy the freshest bread. She could butter it for him. The bakery even sold cake.

The idea of serving his lordship a piece of cake gave her shivers that started in her knees and went up her spine to burst like bubbles somewhere in the region of her heart.

She could serve him cake, and read him *The Wanderer*, and ask what he thought about it and listen. She had the feeling—no, she *knew*—that he'd ask what she thought of the story too.

She'd have more of his kisses. And he could have... anything else he wanted.

When she'd skirted so close to two proposals, her mother had warned her that men wanted their wives to submit to their baser urges like animals in the barn. Nothing had ever sounded less appealing to Isabel.

But if the urges were Lord Hartwick's...

They might even go on walks in Wales someday. Mistresses did that, didn't they?

It was a great deal to contemplate and Isabel felt like she could easily spend another ten years of her life teasing out all the possible details. She could spend another ten years just sitting at this table in this book shop.

But it was growing late, the shop would soon close, and she must make some decisions. Life would not wait forever for her to become whoever she was meant to be. She would have to take action.

"Sir," and with the merest lift of her hand, the shop-keeper was there. He looked desperate for the conclusion of their mutual day. She took pity on him. "My decision. I'll have Mrs. Burney's novel, and *Walks in Wales*. Lady Craven's travel book too, please, and *Waverly*. You said it is popular."

"Indeed, madame." He looked so desperately relieved to finally have her selections. Few customers remained, and likely he had waited for her order hoping his lordship had expensive enough taste that it paid to host this woman in her dull gray coat all this time.

Or perhaps he was simply ready to go home for his own Christmas Eve.

She had made other decisions too. Wales was too forward. The novel was safer. "I want Mrs. Burney's book now, please. I must take it with me."

He tensed. "I have no bound copies at present, madame."

"I'll take the pages."

He stammered that it was irregular even as he led the way back to his small desk. He had already written Lord Hartwick's name on a slip of paper cut there.

And his direction.

All she need do was take the paper. She could read it for herself.

It was a real opportunity. She could take it, and the next steps would be easy. Decision made.

Immediately she doubted that. What would she do, present herself on his doorstep? At the house of his *wife*? And say what?

She swallowed. "The direction—"

"We will deliver the books next week," the bookseller said with determination, wiping a fingertip over one lens of his spectacles. He would not let this sale get away.

"No need," she said quietly. "I shall return for them."

She didn't want oblivion to swallow those books.

She must know for certain that he had them. They were for him. For *them*. When she returned, she would make her way to him. No one had ever needed her before; but he did. Her instinct said so.

Four books was extravagant, but Isabel could not keep shying away from spending others' money or her plan would never bear fruit.

She had no idea what mistresses did, but hazily she perceived that they were supported by their lovers. Jenny would tell. Her family would certainly cut ties with her if they heard about Isabel receiving a man's visits.

She would have to throw herself on Lord Hartwick's mercy.

If he took advantage of her then dropped her, she would be in much more dire straits. Without her father's money she would have to learn a trade to stay alive. The prospect was terrifying.

But not as terrifying as the prospect of counting down her days living a safe life in her safe room all alone.

"As you wish." The bookseller didn't argue. "If you bring back the unbound pages, we'll be happy to bind them for you at another time."

"As long as you don't charge for the binding till it is at

hand." She would have to be a responsible mistress, responsible with his money, with all of him. If she amused him, perhaps she wouldn't have to learn to curb her urge to correct people. Perhaps mistresses were allowed to say what they thought.

"As you say," and he didn't look as happy with his sale now.

Perhaps he suspected her of having some other bookshop do the binding. Perhaps everyone who lived on the generosity of the rich was in the same boat.

She felt much more sympathetic to him then.

Not that he noticed. He finished writing the slip, and Isabel found herself out of doors once more, clutching the unbound sheets of *The Wanderer* to her chest. They were in bunches, folded and tied with string, and the bunches slid as she walked.

Already she had regrets. She should simply have given the shopkeeper her direction. He would have delivered the books to her, all paid for by his lordship, and the whole affair would be concluded. She was no mistress. She could never.

Yet she also had regrets the other way. Why hadn't she simply picked up the paper and read the direction? His lordship had taken a hackney, so his house was not near. But she could have walked. Somehow. Someday. She could have saved another month's pin money and engaged a hackney as well.

This was an agony of freedom.

Torn by competing impulses, Isabel stopped, half desperate to run back inside and simply wrest the direction from the hapless shopkeeper.

Such an action felt as final as running off a cliff.

While she stared into what might have been, a carriage rolled to a stop by the pavement at her feet.

"Bless me, if it isn't the missus!"

"What?" Isabel was startled from her spinning thoughts. If there was one thing she wasn't and would never be, it was a missus.

Above her she saw the same red-faced, round-cheeked driver that had taken Lord Hartwick away.

"'E shouldn'a let you shop alone," said the man with a disapproving *cluck*. "'Tain't right. These young men. Climb in, missus, I'll have you home in a minute."

The possible futures spun faster. "I haven't any coin," she managed to get out, hearing herself sound half-strangled.

"No fear, missus, 'e'll put it right. Climb on in." He lifted his reins as before, when her Lord Mistletoe had rolled away.

She remembered their kiss, and his fear for her safety.

All other possible futures collapsed. Was she really so frightened that it would be better to spend her life alone in those rooms? Forty, sixty more years?

She wasn't afraid of snakes, and she wouldn't be afraid of this.

"Hold fast," she told him. "I will."

A little boy, some street urchin, darted forward between the dangerous wheels to pull down the step before the driver could dismount.

She climbed in and tossed the boy a halfpenny.

"Thank you!" she called back as the cab rolled away, wondering if this adventure would end with her clutching rags around herself, darting between wheels to earn a halfpenny.

She would just have to find out.

CHAPTER 5

The further the carriage went, the finer the buildings became. Gardens appeared behind iron fences, and the buildings grew high, shining white marble in black sky.

Isabel clutched the unbound pages to her chest, needing them for reassurance even as she tried not to crush them.

She must call to the driver to stop. This was exactly what she *must not* do. Lord Mistletoe might want her, but the real Lord Hartwick would not take kindly to her visit; it would fix his impression of her as a beggar, or worse.

And what if she saw Lady Hartwick?

As the wheels rolled on and the buildings grew grander, she settled on plans that quelled her panic.

She *must* see Lady Hartwick. Asking for his lordship at the door would be too presumptuous. And before she tossed away the rest of her morals, she ought to judge for herself whether this marriage was completely unworthy of him.

Because away from his presence, she remembered more of his sunken eyes, the harshness of his approach, the way he'd struck the man who accosted her. Knowing the man for a few hours was not the same as knowing a man all her life. She'd hoped for marriage with two men before and been disappointed; she had better watch her steps, for when she did not even hope for marriage, how might a man like Lord Hartwick disappoint her?

The wheels kept turning and so did her thoughts. He would think the worst of Isabel, appearing on his doorstep; he would not believe her story of the driver. He would think Isabel asked the driver to bring her to his house. Heavens, he might accuse them of conspiring.

The poor driver might end up in gaol.

So might she!

Steadying herself against the carriage with one hand and clutching her pages with the other, Isabel felt a sharp welling of panic.

She stopped it by sucking in a deep breath of cold, damp air. Her heart beat hard in her chest; in fact it was pounding. Nothing had ever made her heart beat this fast before. If she wanted to live a life outside the lines her parents had drawn for her she had better bear up.

Round a lush square of tidy shrubs and cropped green—Isabel could not see the sheep that kept it so, but there must be some—and past a row of tightly built grand houses, the carriage rolled on and on till Isabel feared she was being kidnapped. She might wake up in Scotland. She might wake up on a ship to the Continent.

Or she might not wake up at all.

Finally, after an unbearably long time, finally the carriage rolled to a stop.

Blinking against the dark and the unknown, Isabel opened the door herself.

"I'll help ye, lass, mind the grass," the driver called down, but she was already out. The long hop down to the path jarred her knees and billowed her skirts; hurriedly she shook them down to the dirt path. There were no paving stones here.

She was doing everything wrong already.

That feeling doubled when she hurried forward and put her foot straight into an icy puddle, *plash,* where the hard-packed earth ended and the grass began.

Perfect. A poor woman with a wet, dirty stocking.

Isabel stopped for a moment. She should get right back in the carriage, never mind how to pay for it. She should *walk* back to the center of London, even if the water in her shoe froze her toes solid. She should do anything but knock at the door of a house like this.

It wasn't one of the shining new marble temple-like houses. It was old, its age conveyed by its weathered brick and the ivy draped over its corners. It had gray stone steps that marched in an arc up to its front door and down the other side again and a bewildering array of windows.

And chimneys! Isabel never imagined one house could have so many chimneys.

Well, she couldn't stand here forever and she couldn't walk home. The driver had brought her on a promise of payment, and that payment she must get. Anything else would not be right, no matter how humiliated she felt.

Printed pages flattened to her bosom, she turned and waved upwards. "I'll just be a moment. I must ask at the house for your fare. You've driven such a long way."

He only laughed, his round belly jumping in his coat and his red cheeks glistening from the night-time fog. White curls of hair peeked around the edges of his bowler hat. "It's Christmas Eve, ma'am! Such a sweet little wife oughta be with 'er 'usband on Christmas Eve. Let go whatever might've come between you." He looked up at the brick house-front. "Tell yer man to keep watch on his treasures henceforth."

And with that, he *hy-ucked* the reins, and drove the horses, and the carriage, away.

She thought she knew what panic was. She'd been mistaken. It flooded her now, making her shake from her feet to her hair, as reality bore in upon her and she realized what a fool she had been to climb into that carriage.

Lord Hartwick was likely home, but so would his wife be, and what would she say?

Who would believe a hackney driver would bring her all this way without being paid?

They would take her for an adventuress. Someone bent on besmirching his lordship's name.

Her feet felt like lead as she dragged them up one gray stair, then another. The looming brick wall might topple on her head. She wished it would.

Still searching for a way to explain herself besides her burst of selfish, imagined passion, she pulled the bell rope.

She tried to slow her breathing. It didn't. Her chest heaved as though she had run all the way here.

What would he say? What should she do?

She was no longer concerned with her parents tossing her out of her establishment in Leicester Square. She was concerned with keeping out of prison.

After a million hours of waiting, the door cracked open.

The little maid there, in starched white apron and snowy linen cap, peered suspiciously at her.

Isabel recoiled. The paper pages crinkled against her breast and she had one last coherent thought.

"I've come to deliver a book," she gasped out.

The little maid squinted at her skirts. Isabel refused to look and see if they were splashed with mud, too. She splayed her hands across the tied paper pamphlets.

"You should be round back." The young woman had a slight lisp. "You ought to know that."

"Yes, of course." Desperately Isabel hoped the girl couldn't see how her chest heaved with every fast breath. She'd never minded wearing stays before; they helped support where she was heavy. Now they strangled her. "Should I walk round?" She waved vaguely to one side with the hand that wasn't clutching pages to her chest.

The girl blinked. "Just come through," she whispered as if committing a crime herself.

Terrified that she was about to meet Lady Hartwick in the hall and be surprised in the act of attempting to seduce her husband, Isabel stepped over the threshold.

VICTOR'S MOOD had gone from heavy to foul.

Why on earth had he left the poor girl there in a bookshop alone? Hadn't he already witnessed one man accosting her? How would she travel home after dark? Doubtless walk, given her clothes.

She couldn't have been as luscious as he remembered. In his mind, she took on all the qualities of cake that existed only in dreams. Her smile could not have been as sweet as he remembered, nor her eyes so large. The golden curls that escaped her bonnet could not fall as delicately as he remembered them; nor would it have rewarded him as much as he imagined, had he removed that bonnet and seen their entire glory.

It was only the roundness of her figure that had caught his notice. Hungry as he always was, prickly, uncomfortable, of course he'd noticed a woman whose figure spoke of comfortable ease.

He could easily imagine sinking into the softness of her and never wanting to rise.

Lust. Another burdensome inheritance from his father. Clearly the vice would grow and haunt him till it drove him insane, no matter what he did.

So be it. One more bitter gift from his father's grave.

Such thoughts raked him over and over like poisoned thorns till the butler's interruption was a relief.

"I beg your pardon, Lord Hartwick. There is a caller."

"What?" No one in London knew he was here; and none would bother to call, certainly not at this hour, certainly not on Christmas Eve. "Of course not."

The butler bore being contradicted very well. "As you say, sir."

The quickness with which he turned to go pricked Victor's unease. "What caller?"

"A Miss Snow, she says, sir."

Some lightskirt of his father's. Some actress, with that name, come to find out why his father had stopped sending for her. No lady would drive all the way here this time of night.

His stomach turned. Eating was a trial at the best of times, and now the housekeeper was surly because he'd delayed dinner.

He considered asking the butler for another bottle of liquor. "I don't know any Miss Snow."

"Very good, sir." The butler turned and left him in peace.

Victor closed his eyes and sank back in the heavy leather chair. It stank of whiskey and smoke.

He would wind up just like his father. He abhorred his father's cigars but did sometimes smoke cigarillos. The stim-ulating smoke helped him stay at his work while others refreshed themselves with food he could not eat.

Just like his father's whiskey went down just fine and would help him sleep.

The burn of it felt clean, and fed the spark of life.

He thought again of the woman in the bookshop. Those lips had been so alluring when flushed with the heat of her blood. He couldn't help but wonder if his touch could ever arouse a woman that much. His father had so drummed into him that he was a failure of a man in every way that he had never imagined that he could really do it, that he could satisfy a woman, not with his father's title and money, but with himself. With his body.

Perhaps he ought to cultivate his conversation. The woman in the bookshop who wouldn't give her name had not been bold, but neither had she been terrifically shy. His conversation had been enough to keep her—

He shot to his feet.

The woman in the bookshop had not been bold, but neither had she been shy, and he did not know her name.

"Mr. Cargill!" He ran out down the long corridor as fast as he could. "Mr. Cargill, wait!"

* * *

"IF I MAY JUST SEE Lady Hartwick for a moment."

The lisping maid looked more confused than suspicious now. "What, like, her portrait?"

Having reached the kitchen alive, Isabel's breathing had slowed. Warmth and delicious smells swirled around her but every limb remained tense with the possibility of confronting the less-than-satisfactory Lady Hartwick. "No. I wish to see her."

With wide eyes the girl pointed to the wall. "Churchyard is yonder if you want to wander among the ghosties."

A woman of wide hips and stained apron abandoned her

pot and bustled toward them both. "Alice, don't be foolish. The woman clearly doesn't know." Her soft face turned to Isabel. "She's gone many a year, miss."

"What?" Isabel's glance flicked to the brick wall, then back again. "You mean she's in the... the graveyard?" she whispered.

Just then the butler, a man of narrow shoulders and even narrower eyes, marched back into the kitchen. "His lordship is not at home," he announced briefly before giving the maid a quelling look. "Alice, remember yourself. We know what to do with the women callers."

This straightened the girl's spine. "Oh yes," she said, surveying Isabel's gown and forgetting her fear of ghosts.

The picture kept changing. Poor Lord Hartwick had *lost* his wife. No wonder he was so grim and thin.

Though why he was thin when the kitchen smelled this good still confused her.

Clearly he had many lady callers if the staff *knew what to do*. Isabel flushed. Probably like her, inappropriately late at night.

Her insides steadied and she ignored the squelch in her shoe. It helped that they expected her. She *was* a lightskirt come to visit in the dark of night, and no other woman stood in her way.

Unless he was still caught up in the memory of her.

Though how could he be, if lightskirts were common in the house?

"How many women callers?" she said before she could stop herself.

"Miss Snow." The butler performed a particularly crisp intonation of her name.

Behind him, Alice the maid mimed an explosion with her hands. *Whoosh.*

Did she mean there were *that* many callers? Or was she warning Isabel about the butler's temper?

Or Lord Hartwick's?

The butler didn't see the girl. "We can offer you a plate of supper and then the driver will take you home. Mrs. Reed, will you see to it?"

The cook smiled her pink smile and nodded. "Just you sit here, m'dear, we'll feed you up straight as a ruler."

Isabel did not know what that meant, but she could clearly understand that she was to be fed and sent on her way.

She would never take another chance like this.

She was not ready to let it go.

"But I have a book." The pages rustled again as she clutched them close. Conscious of how she had crushed them for the last half hour, she loosened her grip and tried to slide them back into a semblance of stacked pages. "He wanted—"

"Wanted to be his father after all, apparently," the butler said dryly, and just waved her towards the little table in the corner where the maids clearly had their meals. "He isn't in the mood tonight."

"*The Wanderer*—" She was here. He was here. Somewhere in this house, sad and alone. She could not simply leave him here.

"If you don't wish to eat, I'll have the carriage brought round. Alice, ask Mr. Bottle—"

"I sent Mr. Bottle home." That voice was *him*.

He stood in the doorway. His black coat, his deep-set eyes, all just as stark as she remembered. Unforgiving-looking. Hard.

Yet those tousled curls atop his head and those pillowy lips reminded her of his keen interest, the generosity of his observations, his rare smile.

He looked like he too was breathing a bit heavily. "I was mistaken, Mr. Cargill. I do know Miss Snow. Madame. To what do I owe the honor of this visit?"

She felt the smile spreading over her face. She could not stop it. Seeing him lifted her heart. She had spent many an hour sitting in a parlor with her two previous suitors and never been half so glad to see them.

He was no suitor. He was her ruination. She was so grateful for a real chance to be ruined.

"I brought your book." The words sounded foolish.

But his smile was as sweetly surprised as a little boy's. "Did you, indeed? Impatiently, I see. Mr. Cargill, we'll have supper. In twenty minutes, so Mrs. Hopp may sulk a little first. Miss Snow. May I show you something of the house? I am sad your first visit begins in the kitchen. I assure you the rest of the house is more comfortable."

He offered her his hand.

His smile was like the sun breaking through clouds.

No wonder he was an accomplished rake. It was a heady combination, his darkness and lightness constantly coming and going like quick weather.

She put her gloved hand in his. "Thank you."

The warmth of his touch was not like she had remembered.

It was better.

Isabel found the thought bracing. It would not be pleasure, it would be torture, to feel like this and then miss him for days, perhaps weeks, between visits. Such was the lot of a mistress, she supposed.

But if she forgot a little what it was like to be near him, it would be more bearable when he was away.

He didn't seem to notice the rustling pages clutched to her bosom until she drew near; then he looked down. Isabel stopped breathing.

"Alice," he looked away into the distant corner of the room, neither at her nor the maid, "do take these book pages so Miss Snow may not be burdened with them."

"Oh, no! I mean—I thought we might read them together."

She doubted the word *together* hit him the way it did her. She'd never said such a forward thing in her life.

He smiled down at her, now looking right into her eyes with a kind of heat she had never seen before but still recognized. "Did you?"

CHAPTER 6

*N*one of Victor's past holidays had ever prepared him for one like this.

Her flush was as warm and golden as he remembered. That dreadful coat was gone, yet the plain green gown she wore beneath it was like a brass collar on a diamond. It might protect her, but hardly did her justice.

He didn't want to let go of her hand.

Her fingers were so small. Carefully, he tucked them in the crook of his arm. "Simply say when you are ready to put the pages down, then."

"Of course." She too sounded as if she had been running.

Had she truly just come for the pleasure of his company? Nothing so radical had ever happened to Victor before. He felt an entirely new urge to impress her with this house. *His* house.

The long walk back from the kitchen wing had never been so pleasant. "Henry VIII created the earldom and granted my family the land. It was a country house then. The city has grown around us."

Miss Snow—it felt utterly delightful to know her name—

peered carefully out the windows as they walked down the long corridor back to the house proper. "You have a courtyard."

"Yes, I think my ancestor fancied himself rather Roman. I believe there's still a bit of mosaic under the trees." He shrugged. "There was a fine fountain there when I was a child."

"What happened to it?" She rustled when she walked due to the large collection of tied paper pages hugged to her body. It seemed to serve her as some sort of armor. He longed to relieve her of it.

"I imagine my father disposed of it once my grandfather was dead." He felt that cold wave of fury and helplessness he always did when his father crossed his mind. "He disposed of anything useless."

This was no way to entertain a lady. Victor had only a faint idea how that was done, but this wasn't it.

He pointed out the window again. "There is a Tudor rose engraved on the architraves, above each courtyard door, supported by falcons. The Hartwick crest has falcons."

He wasn't looking at the courtyard, he was looking at her.

Even the colors of her were soft and delicious. Some of the teasing sparkle came back into her eyes. "You did not say you were an earl."

He shrugged. The title chafed, like someone else's coat. "Why would it matter on a walk in Wales?" he asked to defer explanation.

If he told her that those hours spent in a book shop in her company had been the most pleasant of his life, he would appear pathetic.

Her hand spasmed in the crook of his arm; the feeling of it, small, warm, alive, made the whole world feel fresh and joyful.

"I would have expected it to show somehow. Embroidered falcons on your coat, perhaps. Or a vast diamond in the head of your walking stick."

"I have a vast diamond in the head of my walking stick; that is why I left it safely at home."

Her eyes grew even wider. Victor laughed. Actually laughed.

"I have no diamond in my walking stick, Miss Snow."

"Oh!" With one hand in his possession and the other clutching sliding pages of a book, she had no way to wave her hands, but he could see she wanted to. She could have pulled away; she didn't. "That is what finally makes you laugh? To tease me?"

"What else should make me laugh?" He'd learn to laugh if it kept her close.

"No, you're right. I'm a country girl with no Latin or French and I've never been to Wales or anywhere except Allenby's book shop. You *should* laugh if I cannot tell an earl when I see one."

"Well, I've only been an earl for two days." Perhaps that would reassure her.

Instead she stopped, frozen, jaw and arms dropping open, the pages limply sliding to the floor.

"What a fool I am!" It was almost a whisper. "You are in *mourning!* I've disturbed you in *mourning.*"

She seemed to take the idea of mourning much more seriously than he did.

Indeed she seemed stricken. "All in black! Why didn't I notice?"

Victor fought the urge to look down at his clothing.

He always wore black. The coats were serviceable and his peers did the same, even in the Americas, and certainly in Ghent. Most wore fawn trousers, but Victor wore black to hide his lack of bulk.

Gently, so as not to startle her, he slipped to one knee and began picking up the pages.

"Miss Snow. I am entirely grateful for your distraction. I've given no thought to mourning, nor expect to. I plan to mourn my father exactly as much as he would have mourned me." *For about five minutes, later, when it suits me,* Victor thought to himself. "Any distress I feel this evening concerns my work abroad, which I left unfinished to rush to my father's side. In vain."

There. He'd laid some of his pathos out for her to see.

She did not sneer. "What was the work?" was all she said.

So he told her what no one else knew. Because he hadn't conveyed to his father his reasons for sailing directly from Carolina to the Netherlands and had no other family to concern.

He rose before her, the haphazard pile of papers trapped between his palms.

"The treaty with the Americans," he said simply.

"Oh!" She put a great deal of feeling in the wordless sounds she made.

He felt lighter. As if just saying it to someone who didn't throw it back in his face made him taller. Stronger.

"You negotiated a treaty?" She still didn't leave. She seemed... *impressed.*

He hated to disappoint her. "Only consulted on the law."

She did not look disappointed. Her whole face was alight with interest and, yes, admiration. "On the law of a treaty. Imagine that."

It was like opening a floodgate. Things Victor had wanted to tell, wanted to brag about, in truth, spilled from him now, days after arriving at his supposed home.

"I read law with a friend who has since been appointed under-secretary. We both subscribe to the idea of international law, law that transcends boundaries. The world has grown too small for the old law. I went to America to study a problem and he—" Sensing that he was about to pour out the story of his life for the last five years, Victor checked his runaway words. "He asked for my expertise."

"On what?" She looked genuinely interested.

* * *

HE COULDN'T POSSIBLY BE as self-effacing as he appeared. A titled lord, expert in law, called by ministers to consult on a treaty; he had so many reasons to be proud!

And indeed, alight with his topic, the shadow that clung to him faded; he even looked younger.

"The Americans' complaint that we impress their men to sail our ships," he said, simply and clearly as he said every-thing else. The law in his hands must be very clear indeed.

"We do what?" Isabel had never read newspapers. They cost too much for her current living, and when she had been at home her parents had not cared for them. Now she wondered how much she had missed there, too.

"We take their men to sail our ships. We have, I should say, for decades. It was one of the questions of law that vexed me. The Americans want the right to live unmolested by a government they have thrown off, as you might imagine; our courts have time and again upheld our Navy's right to gain men however they can, including taking men from American ships and ports. Under certain circumstances."

He held back again, perhaps aware that he could flood her with information and wanting to spare her. Isabel did not want to be spared.

The world was so large and she had never known anything about it. She could not bear to think how small her existence would have continued had she not decided to buy herself a book for Christmas Eve.

"So you went to look?" She felt stupid asking, but his nod was vigorous.

"I went to look. Two years in Virginia and the Carolinas; Philadelphia too. Some of the legal maneuvering of the Americans was specious—was clearly intended to subvert the law," he added, as if that made it any clearer. Isabel noted to herself what questions she should ask later. "Yet the meat of the thing was clear. Americans *were* removed from the land to staff our ships. Tradesmen, poor men, men of African descent, all forced to sail on our ships." He frowned. "The Americans impressed one of our men as well but that hardly evened the weight of it."

"Please. Let me take back the book." She tugged on the pages. She felt so foolish, having him stand there so serious and holding her unbound pages. The pages she had put on his account.

But he just smiled down at her and shook his head. "I'll have it put in the library. We can read after supper. Ah, Alice."

For the maid bustled down the corridor after them, looking surprised that they had not gone farther.

"Mrs. Hopp says supper is served, sir," said the maid with a little curtsey.

"Fine. Miss Snow, allow me."

THE DINING ROOM was easily the most richly appointed room Isabel had ever seen.

The polished auburn wood of its panels, chairs, and table glowed as if with their own light, and the table's legs were adorned with golden wreaths forming crowns. The snowy linen was set with two places of shining blue porcelain; as Isabel drew closer, she saw the pattern was of deep blue irises. Silver platters and tureens gathered between the two places, and sparkling forks and spoons seemed to be everywhere.

All the glow came to a halt at the black-gowned figure who stood by a sideboard, clutching her hands together at her waist. Isabel thought a gown that black must mean she was mourning many people at once.

"Lord Hartwick." The woman's nostrils flared as if she had been assaulted by some smell.

"Mrs. Hopp." That was all he said, just pulled out the chair at the right of the table's head and gestured for Isabel to sit.

Once he helped her, then seated himself in turn, the crow-like woman took it as a flag to continue speaking.

"The first course is purée of parsnips, beet soup, eggs *à la Française*, roasted partridge, and roasted fennel."

Wet leg forgotten, Isabel's mouth watered. The savory smells seemed to curl from every dish straight to her nose, beckoning, dragging her forward.

One kiss and a faint plan to become a fallen woman, and here she was, slave to the pleasures of her senses.

She was so lost in studying every dainty little dish, all topped with butter in their shining silver haloes, that she failed to notice her companion patiently holding a platter at her elbow.

"My lord! Never wait on me."

"I'm delighted to do it." He looked like he meant it.

The dishes were sufficiently close that they could help themselves, yet he wanted her to have the eggs while they were still warm.

Smiling a little, she helped herself, then sampled a few of the other dishes, only then noticing that his plate held only a roast partridge.

"Have you already eaten?" Surely they would not have waited supper on her.

"No," was all he said.

And as he attacked the partridge, surely no more than six ounces on his plate, Mrs. Hopp approached like a shadow of doom and poured a white sauce from a silver boat over all the remaining birds.

He closed his eyes as if in forbearance and said nothing.

"Let me help you to the parsnips." She scooped some of the creamy vegetables into the ladle in their tureen.

"No." If anything this time it was more short.

"Perhaps the soup."

"No."

Waving to her plate as if inviting her to eat, he himself sliced a small bite of cooked meat from the bird and put it in his mouth.

This was more peculiar than Isabel could bear. "I cannot enjoy all this if you don't join me."

The muscle flexed in his jaw. He looked again like she had first seen him in the bookshop, impatient, angry. "I cannot."

Isabel felt something pulling under her ribs, for him, toward him. He was clearly suffering. "You are ill."

"*No.*" Each time the word was more vehement, more abruptly cut off.

Mrs. Hopp just stood by the sideboard, glaring.

The buttery food suddenly tasted like ashes.

Something was wrong.

Isabel had no idea what a mistress would do. Only the faintest idea what a wife should do.

But she had an impulse that seemed suited to a friend, and she had to follow it.

She had never been able to ignore things that were wrong.

"Would you excuse me a moment?"

Confused, her host paused in demolishing his lone, small bird, and just nodded. Frustration emanated from him so strongly she could feel it, frustration and embarrassment.

Mrs. Hopp just watched her like an angry vulture.

She would hurry.

* * *

It took only moments to rush down the long corridor they had strolled so slowly before.

"Mrs. Reed." In the kitchen, Isabel went right to the cook, who was bent over a delicious-smelling roast of beef. "His lordship only took one partridge. Can you give him another?"

"I sent out four!"

"Mrs. Hopp poured sauce over them and..." She didn't explain how she knew he would not take another. She just knew. "Is he ill? Please tell me. I know you did not cook all this for me."

The face of the friendly cook gyrated through anger and embarrassment herself, then back to anger. "It's not right of her to do that."

"What? Please tell me." His lordship was so young. Did he suffer from a wasting disease? A cancer? Isabel had to know. He was too young, and too brilliant, for such an end.

"T'owd master set his menu, and t'new lad hasn't had a minute to talk to her since he returned. Or mebbe avoiding her. I would if I could." She saw Isabel's continued confusion and added, "That harpy serves t'owd master's dinners knowing young master can't eat it. She's 'eartless, she is."

"But why can he not eat it?"

Mrs. Reed just shrugged her round shoulders under her apron. "Never could. Every dinner a battle! The earl insisting him eat what he got or nothing, the lad picking out a dry bit here and there. It's heartless." Then she patted Isabel's hand with her own strong one. "Never you fear. I always sent him some plain bread later. And apples. Raw scraped carrots, if you can believe."

Isabel didn't understand any of this, but the important thing seemed clear. "Then do it now!"

"Mercy, yes." She half-turned to her pots, then hesitated. "You'll... he won't let t'owd harpy sack me?"

Isabel understood that cooks were subject to the rule of housekeepers, but why hadn't Lord Hartwick's wife done something about this while she was alive?

Heavens, had the housekeeper *killed* the woman?

There was no time to feel faint again. This Isabel must manage. "There's nothing else for it. We cannot let him starve. Take a slice or two of that roast to a skillet and make it brown, please, Mrs. Reed. Bring that out on its own platter, dry as you can, and another plate with some of that bread. Does he eat butter?"

"No, miss." Mrs. Reed looked pleased with her cheeks but frightened with her eyes.

"Have you anything else you know he can eat?"

"The seed cake, ma'am. He loves his cake. I give him some for breakfast."

As if she'd snuck keys into a dungeon.

What ailed this housekeeper?

"Very well." Isabel cast another sharp eye around the room. "Bring some cheese—*don't* toast it, bring it cold—and one of those apples. In fact, give me those and the bread now. Bring the beef and cake when you can."

She had already left him alone for long minutes. Whatever he thought of her, he must think her peculiar already; this would hardly lessen the impression.

Still, she carried the little platter out of the kitchen herself.

Only to find, waiting outside the door, Mrs. Hopp.

The ghastly woman trembled with rage like a black ribbon in an invisible wind. "That is not your place."

For the first time Isabel wanted not just to correct, but to scold. "It cannot be your place to starve the Earl."

She scoffed. *Scoffed.* "As if he will ever be that. A willful brat taking the first chance he has to sully his father's legacy. He knows perfectly well his father would never allow him to eat bread and apples at the table like a servant boy. He was a silly child and still is. Nor did his father let tarts dine at table." She seized Isabel's upper arm in a claw-like grip.

The accoster in the bookshop had been frightening because he had been bewildering. This woman was all too easily understood. "Let go of me!"

"You march right back in that kitchen and—*owp*."

The noise was because the housekeeper's wrist had been engulfed in a much larger hand.

"Mrs. Hopp." One by one he peeled the woman's claws from Isabel's arm. "You are discharged."

Like a cart rolling downhill, the housekeeper couldn't seem to change her direction. "Your father tried so hard to make a lord of you!"

"And now he's dead." He still stood over her, all implacable shadow. He let go her hand as if it were a poisonous spider, remained rooted between her and Isabel.

His voice was as calm and clear as ever; so were his words. "I don't mind your scorn. I don't like you either. But you will not touch Miss Snow again. You're discharged."

"*Miss*," spat the older woman. "Tarts should know to use the servants' entrance and not to sit at table." Then the meaning of his words seemed to penetrate her seething anger and she subsided like a squashed pile of hay. "Discharged?"

"Discharged. And my tarts may use whatever door they like."

Mrs. Hopp gasped as if seeing him for the first time. "A puppy playing the dog," she retorted weakly, watching him warily. "Though more like him every day, it seems."

That made his lordship wince again but he did not answer the jibe. "I arranged a pension for you at the solicitor's yesterday. I intended to wait to discharge you till after Christmas. Merely a courtesy recognizing your years of service to my father. You've never served me." He held out his hand. "Your keys, please."

She made no noise about Christmas or mercy. Isabel melted inside for the little boy who had essentially been raised by this woman. She only said, "I expected as much."

"I imagine you would." His fingers wrapped around her surrendered chain of keys. He stayed where he was, between Isabel and the housekeeper, and raised his voice rather than take two steps into the kitchen. "Mrs. Reed?"

"Yes, my lord?" The woman had clearly hidden just around the door jamb, hanging on every word.

Isabel had the feeling she was witnessing the resolution of some very long-standing feuds.

Lord Hartwick handed the housekeeper's keys to the cook. "Fetch a footman and confine Mrs. Hopp to her room. She's leaving us tomorrow. No one need interrupt their Christmas Eve to escort her anywhere."

"Yes, sir." Mrs. Reed didn't even try to hide her glee.

Mrs. Hopp regained enough poise to look down her nose at Isabel, then at his lordship. "Your father knew how to follow the rules of decent society. He tried to teach you. You have no self-control at all. You're a demon run free."

Lord Hartwick did not answer. He turned to Isabel as if no one else existed. "Would you care to resume our meal, Miss Snow?"

Stunned out of her silence, still clutching her small platter, Isabel's answer felt inappropriate; but in the face of Mrs.

Hopp's vile accusations, she was perfectly willing to be inappropriate. "Whatever you'd like."

"Very good. If I may." And he took the silver platter from her hands.

Without anything to hold, she wanted to cling to his arms, but restrained herself.

By the time they reached the end of the long corridor they heard the hard-hearted housekeeper exchanging bitter words with two young footmen who'd already had a few ales and seemed to find her predicament hilarious. Isabel did not fear she would be contained.

But she did not find any of the situation hilarious.

Lord Hartwick simply walked her back to the dining room, where he sat again at the table and began to slice the apple she'd brought.

Only then did he look her way, with an echo of the wince she now knew was from an inner hurt. "I apologize. You should never have been subjected to the woman."

"Nor should *you*! Why on earth would she feed you this way?" Whatever his illness, Mrs. Reed knew what to do; Isabel could not imagine a reason not to let her do it.

In fact, at that moment Mrs. Reed appeared, carrying two slices of dry beef on a platter and a small plate of cake.

Lord Hartwick's little noise of unrepentant pleasure tugged at Isabel everywhere.

And Mrs. Reed made clear she would continue to serve her new lord. "Good for you, sir," she whispered, bending near as she placed the food at his elbow before disappearing herself. "Never you fear, Mr. Cargill will see she's gone tomorrow without pocketing any of the silver."

"I don't care about the silver," he muttered but gave a short nod indicating he heard and understood. He sliced off a bite of the beef before she had even closed the door.

"Apologies," he said again to Isabel when his mouth was empty, as if he had something to apologize for.

"You need not apologize to anyone." Isabel felt incensed at him on his own behalf, watching him take a bite of the cake. "But if I may ask. Why allow her to treat you so?"

He sighed, swallowing his cake like a starving man. Which he must be. "Habit, I suppose." He looked so embarrassed Isabel wanted to pet his hand, but would not while it was still applied to the important business of eating. "I have only been home two days. Word reached me in Ghent that my father was ill, and I was persuaded to respond. I rushed to a Flemish port by carriage and sailed to London as quickly as I could. The vessels are all packed with wounded men coming home. Never travel with hundreds of desperate men, Miss Snow. The smell, the noise, are incredible.

"When I arrived home all was just as I had left it, except my father was dead... twelve hours before I arrived. All my effort, wasted."

He looked like he wanted to throw the food in his hand, but set it down on the plate instead, scowling, before going on.

"Wasted like my life. I wanted to help bring peace with America. I spent years traveling and listening to the stories of wives and children the impressed men left behind. I could not help them. Many of their men died on the high seas. No one ever even notified the women."

His hands flattened at the sides of his plate. "Then we war with them over the right to do that. Americans and British alike, slaughtered at Detroit and Lake Erie. Their new capital, burned. I had no reason to leave America, Miss Snow, yet no way to help. Till the under-secretary's letter found me there. I left directly, I was so determined to help settle this war.

"Then my father's illness called me away when we were

so close, *so close* to signing. Now the only news I have is what the papers print, and they say both sides are perfectly willing to go on killing in this thrice-bedamned war!"

He looked about, as if for something to throw.

"I am a useless man who has lived a useless life."

"Not so! *Not* so." Even if Isabel were inclined to let mistakes pass by, she would not let him think so ill of himself. She had just seen his upbringing in miniature, and it clearly still burdened him. "Who else took it upon themselves to find out the truth? Who else took so much action? You saw a wrong and you wanted to right it. That is, to my mind, the best sort of man."

He looked at her, some quirk of expression flitting around his face, and all she could see was the square set of his jaw and the pursing of his lips. His face gave none of his thoughts away.

CHAPTER 7

$\mathcal{I}$f Victor did not put more distance between them he would do something dastardly. "Do you like this room, Miss Snow?"

"It is the most beautiful room I've ever seen," she told him frankly.

"It's shiny." He shrugged it away. "Would you be willing to adjourn elsewhere? For I admit the room does nothing for me."

Every hour since he'd returned had offered some new humiliation, and now tonight he had survived a veritable bouquet of them. She had seen his weakness, not just before food but before the memories he was unable to banish.

For two days this had still been his dead father's house. Mrs. Hopp had been mourning, not beside his father's shrouded body, but in a parlor downstairs surrounded by family portraits and silver. He suspected the legacy of this title meant far more to her than him.

He'd had the corpse removed to the local church. They'd buried it yesterday, in a cloth-covered coffin decorated with nails. Victor had not held a funeral.

Perhaps that was why he felt every room of the house was haunted by memories of his father belittling him, taunting him, and yes, starving him.

Victor remembered when food had begun to revolt him. He didn't know why his very bones rebelled at the thought of putting it in his mouth, much less swallowing it. He knew it was a weakness, yet he could not simply overcome it at his father's orders.

He could stay awake and alert without food, as his father had forced him to do many times, sometimes for days. But he could no more eat watery eggs than he could fly.

He glanced at the platter of scrambled eggs *à la Française*. It repelled him.

He ought to have given orders about the meals. He was too used to hiding in his room with bread and fruit. In America, in Ghent, he'd simply paid to have provisions brought and fed himself. Rarely was he able to get a piece of meat cooked to his satisfaction, but it had not been impossible.

He'd never felt like Hartwick's heir, nor did he feel like an earl now. He'd eaten edges of the food served last night and not taken the time to wrangle with Mrs. Hopp before going into the city today to see a solicitor and find a newspaper.

Dismissing her would not change the tenor of the house; all the servants gave him odd looks. They always had and always would. But there were more people in the world than just himself.

He had not acted quickly, and so he was indirectly responsible for the kindest, loveliest lady being subjected to vile abuse. As if she were the kind of midnight tart his father had ordered to the house the way he ordered kegs of ale.

Miss Snow was a lady, whatever her circumstances, and he was not like his father.

And she was so indulgent. "I'll dine anywhere you like.

But as the food is laid here, perhaps you would be willing to eat here briefly, then adjourn wherever you'd prefer?"

To bed, was his immediate silent thought. God, she was beautiful, she was kind, and she was *luscious.* He wanted every part of her more than he had ever thought possible.

It had not been difficult to play the monk to his father's libertine. Women were suspicious of a man who would not dine with them, and he had no model on how to speak to them but his father's.

This woman was easy to speak with, to dine with, and he suspected she would be even easier to lay with.

She mistook his silence. "I suggest finishing the meal here only from a care for the servants. They must already carry everything back to the kitchen, and it is Christmas Eve."

"That it is." He'd forgotten again. Now he felt like celebrating. "Let me ring for someone."

"I'm right here, my lord, right here." Mrs. Reed, the cook, hurried through the door as if she had been hiding behind it the whole time.

It didn't matter. Victor felt light. He could do anything with the household that he pleased. These were his servants. This was his house.

It was his title, and it belonged to him.

For the first time he could imagine doing something with it.

"Mrs. Reed." He felt almost giddy. Giddy wouldn't do. He tried to behave soberly. "Please bring a platter of all the choicest bites to the library and have Mr. Cargill add a bottle of claret. Miss Snow and I will not require anything else, and the rest of the dinner may go to the kitchen for anyone celebrating Christmas Eve."

"Yes sir," she said smartly, and curtsied. "And my lady."

The lady sat straight in her seat. "I am only Miss Snow."

She was a by-God angel. And he had neglected to see to

her. So light did he feel, freed of the weight of disapproval that pressed on him in this house, he felt ready and able to do anything. He would certainly see to her now.

"Yes, ma'am." Mrs. Reed bustled out looking smug, of all things.

It must not have been pleasant serving under Mrs. Hopp.

"Very well. Shall we retire?" He heaped the rest of his food on his plate and swept it up with one hand, offered his elbow to Miss Snow as she rose.

"You ordered a choice platter for the library."

"For you," he explained, keeping hold of his plate. He noticed that somewhere in there, he'd finished the cake.

She copied him, picking up her plate and fork in one hand, slipping the other into the crook of his arm. "Lead on," she said with a twinkle in her eye that betrayed the adventurer hidden in the guise of a meek little woman.

He did.

It felt entirely different to show the house to someone as if it were his. It *was* his. "The music room has an excellent pianoforte. I prefer it to the harpsichord."

"Do you?" She peeked inside for only a moment, choosing to stay by his side.

He found it an intoxicating habit.

The hallway was lined with oil paintings collected by his grandfather and great-grandfather, weapons mounted on plaques, and a few old tapestries succumbing to moths. He should do something about those, he thought.

Everything in this house was his.

Except her.

"Do you like to dance? There is an excellent dancing studio." He stopped that train of thought. His father had only known two kinds of women: the kind with high noses and high titles, and the kind whose blouses somehow managed to fall off when they lifted their arms. Neither would be suitable company for Miss Snow should the new Earl of Hartwick arrange a ball.

Though if he chose, he could do that.

A ball would be packed with sorbets and trifles and other things he could not eat; but this was his house.

Miss Snow might enjoy that.

Whole futures of possibility fanned out before him like the loose pages Miss Snow had brought. Mrs. Reed could feed him aside; he need not force himself to try sorbets. Who would question what he did in his own home? If his father could tyrannize, so could he.

Then he realized tyranny would be forcing everyone to eat the same dry bread and meat he preferred. He suppressed a smile.

There was so much to show her. The stables, the rookery, everything. "The courtyard is a bit small for pall-mall games, but the garden at the rear of the house is wider. Do you enjoy hunting?"

"What, with pistols?" She did not look alarmed, only curious.

"With falcons. Many of the ladies hunt by falcon. There is still quite a bit of game in this area."

"I've never tried."

* * *

INDEED, Isabel had never heard of such a thing.

The farther they went into the house, with every new amusement he mentioned, she thought over and over to herself, *I would be the most boring mistress in the history of Britain.*

Clearly the business of amusing people was extensive.

Until she moved to London, Isabel's idea of risk had been sewing cross-stitch patterns without drawing them first.

The risk tonight had come out of worry for Lord Hartwick, and it had clearly paid. He looked younger, happier, his deep-set eyes more relaxed; she could see now, when they passed lit candles, that his eyes were a beautiful mix of sea green and golden brown.

She could easily spend an hour simply staring at them and tracing their patterns. Food was no longer so necessary. Nothing was, really.

It was easy to ignore how clearly he knew her station. He spoke and led her through the house familiarly, as if they had been childhood friends, but without consciousness that they were alone. Obviously he did not want a chaperone. Isabel didn't either.

When her mother had insisted on remaining in the parlor when her suitors came to call, she'd given Isabel the unseemly impression that had she not been there, one or the other man would have fallen upon her neck and possibly rent her throat.

She'd once had the sensation with Mr. Wheelock that it was true.

But here there was no chaperone. She was thoroughly compromised, unsuitable for marriage to a curate with a nice little house near the church; since that had previously been her life's aspiration, she had nothing left to want.

Except the feel of this man's arms around her.

She wondered again about the last Lady Hartwick. Had he been in love with her? How had they not had children? For surely if he had them, he would have mentioned them by now.

Did he already have another mistress? One who took no interest in his well-being, only... well, only pleasured him in bed?

Was that what he liked?

Such questions plagued her as they wandered about the

great house, Isabel only half-hearing details of this room dating to that king or what the peculiar felt-covered tables in the gaming room were for.

After what felt like long wanderings, they reached the library.

Isabel had expected it to feel as comfortable as the book shop. But it was entirely different. In the shop, books had been dismembered, only the samples bound in cloth and boards in order to be touched along with the leather, watered papers, and gilt a person could select for their own volume.

Here, richly finished volumes marched in ranks along oak shelf after oak shelf, facing each other across the room like soldiers. The rest of the room reflected the age of the house, polished, its plastered ceiling criss-crossed with dark planks. One supported a vast crystal chandelier.

Isabel could not stop staring at the glittering arrangement of crystal. "Could it fall?"

"Doubtful. Does it alarm you?" Lord Hartwick barely spared a glance at the thing, only rose to move their little serving table and plates out from under it. When she drew near, he turned a plush chair to give her a more comfortable seat.

"Not alarm. Awe," she told him honestly.

He sat across from her, his hand carelessly plucking morsels of food from his plate. Isabel imagined it wandering as carelessly over her skin, and felt her belly tighten.

She no longer feared submitting to a man's baser impulses.

She had never before felt these sensations in her skin, in her fingertips. Her damp stocking was forgotten; all her skin felt warm. She longed to touch the curve of his lip; it called to her, she could barely take her eyes from it.

But she also wanted to feel his hands on her shoulders, on

her back, on her breasts. She had never wanted such a thing before. Now the soft skin there positively ached for his notice. She was burning for him to touch her.

It frightened her, but it proved second by second that she had made the right choice.

She could never be the mistress of a home like this, but of him? That she could do.

The only problem now was she had no idea what a mistress would say.

"Ah." He reached with a long arm to an ancient oak sideboard. "And here are your pages, Miss Snow. You've been so kind to attend to my supper, let me entertain you while you eat yours."

"Reading while dining?" It felt almost as scandalous as what she imagined him doing with his lips. "I've never heard of such a thing."

His gaze flicked to her face, then dropped to her plate. "It is a day for discovery," was all he said, before he skipped to the paragraph where she had paused in the bookshop and began to read.

It felt as intimate as an embrace from an old friend.

* * *

VICTOR HAD NEVER ATTEMPTED to entertain anyone by reading. But Miss Snow deserved the effort.

He tried to vary his voice with the rising and falling of the story, sounding as lively as he could. He tried to keep his eyes on the printing, but couldn't help watching her savor every bite she put in her mouth. He saw it even when he wasn't looking; the vision of her lips closing around the tines of the fork etched itself indelibly on the back of his eyelids, in the depths of his brain, and indeed around the base of his spine.

It spread heat across his belly till he was glad he should not have to stand up.

The exhaustion of the past months of hard work and then days of panicked travel caught up with him. He let it peak and run out of him like water. There was no past, no future; only this bright moment here with this sweet woman, who listened so attentively to his voice.

Her lips parted. So divided was his attention between her and the page that he saw it instantly. He paused.

A little frown drew her brows together. She said, "Go back to the beginning. Where they were wondering if she spoke English."

"You've forgotten already?" He knew he sounded too severe, too dry, for proper wit.

But she seemed to understand his mood. Her own quiet smile appeared and disappeared. "The section haunts me. I wonder if I heard correctly."

The loose pages flapped in his hands; he had to curve them back upon themselves to keep them firm enough to read.

"You must resign your demoiselle, as Mr. Riley calls her, for a heroine," whispered the young lady to Mr. Harleigh. *"Her dress is not merely shabby; 'tis vulgar. I have lost all hope of a pretty nun. She can be nothing above a house-maid."*

"She is interesting by her solitary situation," he answered, *"be she what she may by her rank; and her voice, I think, is singularly pleasing."*

"Oh, you must fall in love with her, I suppose, as a thing of course. If, however, she has one atom that is native in her, how will she be choked by our foggy atmosphere!"

He had passed by the similarities when reading, but now her interest in the passage was clear.

"And is it so?" Miss Snow said when he paused, wondering what to say to reassure her without being a cad.

"Is what so?" He needed more time to think.

"Any solitary woman is interesting."

He could try joking again. "Certainly if she cries out in agony on a beach in the middle of the night during the Terror."

Her fleeting smile appeared and disappeared again, but she persisted. "Is that all that caused him—or rather you—to speak to me in that bookshop?"

His inclination to smile faded as well. "A villain accosted you."

"And you pretended to be a husband with ownership of me. I do not complain!" she rushed to add. "You surely understand that my life will go on after this day, and I would simply like to understand. Is it true that I should expect accosting whenever I walk out of doors alone?"

Victor had to think. His instinct was to reply as clearly and honestly as a good contract. But contracts existed to put both parties on equal footing, and as a woman, his guest could not assume she would get that.

The whole affair was too far from his experience for him to say anything useful.

More than anything, he wished she would not associate him with the other man in the shop, that she had only met *him*.

The thing was impossible.

He'd rebuffed the other man out of his own ire, his own need to appear righteous.

A righteous sham. For right here, right now, he wanted to sweep this woman into his arms and devour the taste of every inch of her skin and do exactly the things other men wanted. He wanted it all, crowned with her willing, enthusiastic cries. He was not sure himself how different he was from his father, or any other man right now.

He could not admire these wild yearnings, so base; yet they were his. He was not so worthy.

"The shopkeeper mistook us for married," prompted Miss Snow, "and forced you into the pantomime. Was that the difference? The other man's interest was crude, but yours merely a game?"

Victor frowned. Glanced at the bottle of claret between them. It was still full, still bore its crystal stopper. He wished for a bit of its support right now. His childhood had wrapped him in an icy shroud of indifference supported with the drugs of tobacco and alcohol. He longed to shed them. But to become what kind of man?

"Madame." He turned his plate. "A game, like a contract, is the meeting of two equal parties. In no way was that man my equal." The moment he said it, Victor realized it was true. He could have simply turned the man away, rebuffed him as an equal would. Something in *him* had driven him to claim ownership of his Miss Snow. He had wanted the toothsome cake of a woman, and claimed her.

He *was* a ruffian.

But he had given her the grace to rebuff him. That at least was to his credit. It was her disadvantage, as an interested party, that she must perforce wait for such grace to be given.

But he had extended that grace, and she had *not* turned him away.

He hadn't thought of that before.

Trying to sound warm, he added, "I enjoy conversation with you."

God, now he was both pathetic and stuffy.

He *must* explain himself better. "I am no gamesman. If I were, what points were mine? If I rescued you, you came here and rescued me and won the point back."

They exchanged a look that spoke of a shared moment in time. He had never had that with anyone before.

It emboldened him to go on. "I liked talking with you. I offered you a disguise, not a game. And I enjoyed it. No! Never worry."

For she hid her face behind her hands. "I played it like a game."

Without noticing himself, Victor vaulted from his chair to kneel by hers. It would be too forward to touch her hands, and he was trying to prove himself *not* a ruffian, but he wanted to. Wanted to kiss her knuckles, one by one, till her hands fell away and he could touch her face. "It had to be your game because I do not know how to play."

He had never had a playmate, or a lover, or even a friend.

Right now he could only imagine one person filling all those roles. He could not remember a time before he knew this woman.

Trying not to alarm her with his nearness yet unable to move away, when she did not speak, he went on as best he could. "You made it easy for me to stay by your side, and I was so grateful, because I wished to be there. Leaving you was so incredibly difficult."

She peeked through her hands. Her eyes were large, the gray in them bright in the candlelight. She pressed her fingers to her lips. He wondered if those impossibly small fingertips were rough. He wanted to touch them and find out for himself.

As if she heard his thoughts, she touched one fingertip to *his* lips, silencing him as she had silenced herself.

Victor had to fight to keep his eyes from drifting closed with the pleasure of that one soft touch.

Her voice was faint in that way he'd already come to realize meant she was forcing out each difficult word. "Is that what you liked in your wife? Conversation?"

"What wife? I have no wife." *Please keep touching me.*

"I know, but when you did."

She sounded so certain. When did she hear this lie?

"Madame." Addressing her that way when they were a hands-breadth apart was ridiculously formal, but his speech was his speech. "We have not been introduced. I am Victor Adell, Earl of Hartwick for perhaps seventy-two hours. And you are?"

"Miss Isabel Snow," she said quietly, eyes darting around his face as if trying to divine the rules of their new game.

But Victor was done with games.

"Ah. Isabel is a lovely name." Did he sound like a cad? He was driving himself mad. "Perhaps you will accompany me." He stood and offered his hand.

She rose and took it.

In contrast to their chattering earlier tour, this time he led her in silence.

The wide sweeping staircase had been built for crowds of courtiers in panniers, the processionals of dukes and kings.

Three hundred years of earls had led their ladies up these stairs, and Victor felt the weight of that history for the first time as he led Miss Isabel Snow the same way.

His father must have felt this moment very differently. He had yoked himself to a wife for money and influence, and said so openly of her, alive or dead.

That man had never led a woman upstairs he might love, because he had never been capable of loving.

Perhaps Victor could behave differently.

The carpet in the upper halls was a bit worn, but still colorful. It brightened the heavy wood walls. Victor wanted to ask if Miss Snow cared for them. Would she prefer one of the new houses with soaring marble pillars? He wanted to know.

But they had other matters to settle first.

The great chamber was to his left; he turned away from it. There his father had lived and died.

Instead he turned to the massive chamber on the right, the one that looked out on the front lawns and thence to the modern new road along their edges.

Miss Snow said nothing as he opened the ancient iron-bound door and led her within.

"Here," he said, waving his hand past the small fire and the furnishings to the wall ahead, "is the last Lady Hartwick."

Slowly, Miss Snow walked to the vast portrait.

It stretched from floor to ceiling. The lady within was dark-haired, like Victor, with the same serious brow and firm chin. Her eyes were a little too deeply-set to be called strictly pretty. They looked even more incongruous under her vast pink wig and wide ruffled gown.

But her intelligence was obvious.

"My mother died when I was young. I have never married."

His guest examined the grand portrait the same way she examined books. Slowly, taking her time to absorb the details.

Finally she turned back to Victor. Those soft, bright eyes had a look in them now that was much more personal. She knew things about him. "I'm sorry that happened to her. And to you."

He wanted to know so many private, personal things about her.

CHAPTER 8

Isabel felt her heart soar, then sink.

He had no wife. She would not encroach upon any other woman's rights by attempting to fascinate him.

But neither could she ever be that woman in the portrait.

She was a plump, plain pubkeeper's daughter, and she had never been angrier with her parents than in this moment, when she keenly felt that they had never prepared her to do anything more than wait upon a curate.

Though could schooling make Isabel into a woman like that? She thought not. That lady seemed to be a completely different kind of creature. She must have walked among so many very highly-born people, educated, distinguished, with titles and power; people who wore diamonds and played pianos. People like Victor Adell, Lord Hartwick.

People who would look at Isabel like the accoster in the shop had. Like Mrs. Hopp had.

Isabel looked again at the lady with grand skirts and keen eyes. "She must have imagined you as you are now. Using your intelligence. Being a better man than your father."

He straightened, clearly startled. Had no one ever paid this man a compliment? He studied the portrait too.

What did he see? The choices of all the earls who had gone before him? Or the mother he never knew?

Even the idea of being part of such a long family legacy exhausted Isabel. She had barely met her grandparents. They were farmers in the north, near Sheffield. Tenant farms, she now realized. Likely tenants of a man much like the one beside her now.

She had come here to be a mistress, but she was not grand enough even for that.

Isabel wanted to press him on the answers to all her questions. What he liked in a woman. Why he had stayed with her in the bookshop. Whether he intended to marry, and did he know who that would be.

But she was suddenly tired, so tired, all the hours and ups and downs of the day weighing on her along with a keenly inward-cutting disappointment she no longer had the strength to put aside.

"I am keeping you awake, Lord Hartwick. You must want sleep."

He scowled and winced at once, and she knew he was berating himself for something. How easy it had become to know his inner movements in only a few hours.

"Unforgivable of me. Here I am keeping you awake into the small hours. You must bathe and sleep."

"I can sleep in the library." For it had a comfortable settee, and all Isabel wanted now was a little sleep and to slip away unnoticed in the morning.

"Nonsense. I was the fool for dismissing the servants to their holiday when you still have needs. You shall sleep here."

"I couldn't!" She could not. The grand lady would haunt her all night, taunting her with a life she was unprepared to imagine, much less live.

"You must." With that simplicity that brooked no disagreement, he was gone.

Isabel's nerves still hummed, but she truly did feel exhausted, body and spirit. She perched on the edge of the great bed, marveling at its carved oak posters and the ranks of damask curtains ready to enclose whoever lay there.

Toppling over, she rested her head on the cushions.

A warm smell rose from the heavy fabric, a smell composed of paper and sealing wax and roast almonds and skin.

This was his bed.

She ought to spring upright, but she curled in closer. There was no doubt he slept here. She did not know when in this long, long day she had become familiar with his scent. Perhaps in the book shop when he had looked over her shoulder at pages. Perhaps over supper, when he had urged her to add more butter to her plate. Perhaps just now in the library.

It had wound around the core of her and would never let go.

It seemed like only moments before his lordship reappeared, two long chains slung over a yoke on his shoulders bearing sloshing, steaming full buckets. They splashed his trousers.

Isabel sprang up. "You shouldn't have!"

He shrugged it away. "I do not like to go back on my word. I gave the servants their Christmas holiday, so I thought I would bring you this myself."

He filled the washbasin by the fire and moved a stool to stand near, piled high with clean linens and an open box holding a bar of soap.

A faint wisp of almond scent from it reached her.

They had shared so many intimacies already. Some

awkward, some cutting deep. Perhaps he was as exhausted as she.

Isabel could not bring herself to say aloud that she knew this room was his.

She tried not to feel awkward. The house was huge. He would find somewhere to rest. But it would be awkward nonetheless, sleeping in linens that smelled of him.

"Thank you." She could barely get out the words.

Someday he would have a wife, a lady who would speak confidently. Wisely, perhaps even about the law. His wife would know important people and how to entertain them in every room of this abundant house.

"What else would you like?" He seemed as serious about that as about everything else. "Are you still hungry? Perhaps a glass of claret would help you sleep. You should have one—I'll fetch one."

And with that he left her next to a basin of steaming water beside the fire in the lady's chamber.

Isabel had come with the intention of seducing him. How foolish that felt now. Not only could she not fill the role, she was almost too shy to unfasten her gown, even without him in the room.

Everything here breathed of his presence, all the more palpable because he was not actually here. She could breathe in the scent of him as deep as she liked without his notice. It only intensified her longing for a glimpse of the base of his throat.

Sighing, Isabel unbuttoned her shoes and rolled down her wool stockings, laying them on the hearth where they would dry the quickest and she could brush away the mud.

Only then did she untie the ribbons that held up her gown in front and around the waist. It folded and fell down around her feet, a puddle of plain green wool amidst all this grandeur. Her stays and chemise followed.

The glow of the fire made the water look like molten gold. Isabel laid folded linen on the uncarpeted spot near the fire clearly left bare for this purpose and dipped a smaller cloth and the thick bar of soap into the water, making it ripple.

The soap lathered creamy white almost with a touch. With the washing cloth she smoothed it up her arms, around her neck, even over her face, then dipped another in the bucket beside her to rinse the suds away. The stain of mud along her leg disappeared.

It felt rather wicked and peculiar, yet luxurious, to wash herself here in this strange room, bare to her toes. She did not have the prize she came for; yet she bathed as if she belonged here, as if she was the mistress, if not of him, then at least of this tub.

The crisp linens, hot and soft with water, and the soapy trails they left behind lit a fire underneath her skin, reminding her that she was bare, and had come for his touch.

They forced her imagination onward when she would hold it back, making her swell in places she wanted to calm, making it even more awkward to wash her own golden curls and the crevices that never saw anyone's attention but hers.

She had come for him to touch her there. The thought coalesced as she washed herself slowly, tender in places still lonely for his attention. She had come to be wanton, that was all.

Such a small thing, yet so huge in her imagination.

There was now an entire new dimension to the loneliness of the rest of her life. Not only would she never have a home of her own or children, she would never know what it would be like for his wide, blunt hands to stroke her here, and here.

She would never know what it would be like to please him, or for him to please her.

She had not dared to imagine it before, but it was impossible not to imagine now. Had she been someone different, dared something different, he could have leaned her back on that soft bed and touched her soft secret places and she would swell for *him.* She had no idea what it would be like, but she did not have to imagine wanting it desperately.

She already did.

If he were here, in this room, watching her now, she would not have to speak. If only he could see her now, her fantasies would come true.

* * *

VICTOR INTENDED to dash away and bring her the promised glass of claret. It bothered him not to do as he said he would do. He didn't consider it firmness of character, only the bare agreement of civilized life: for men to do as they promised.

Yet despite all that, he lingered.

He told himself it was in case she needed help. Perhaps to lift a heavy bucket.

But truth was, he did not wish to go.

Pressing his ear to the door was unforgivably intrusive, proving him just the ruffian he most hoped not to be.

But his bad behavior was rewarded with the soft sound of a sigh, and his good intentions were undone.

He wanted to hear more. He could faintly imagine the softness of her lips, her skin everywhere, the brightness of her hair shining against the velvet of her skin.

If he had ever doubted he could want to hold a woman the way other men did, those doubts were gone now.

If ever he were to take that leap, it had to be now. It had to be the one woman he had ever met who seemed gentle enough to forgive him any shortcomings, yet curious enough to try.

Her lips would taste of butter. His eyes closed and he gave

up any pretense of civility. He spread his fingers against the heavy wood of the door, wishing it thinner, listening hard.

It might have been his imagination, but he thought he could hear quiet sounds of sloshing water. Her hands in the basin, on the soap. His soap.

The swelling length that made his trousers uncomfortable turned hard as stone at the thought.

He wanted everything about him all over her. His lips. His hands. His skin leaving its scent on hers, and vice versa.

He had starved for food so much of his life, yet it was this hunger that would kill him.

His hand drifted up to the aching hardness before him and pressed it down. Far from making it subside, it swelled.

Another sloshing sound from inside. Imagining the wet peach-pink flush of her skin, he rubbed himself harder.

Of course she did not want a man like him. She had seen his faults first-hand, and his weaknesses. He would never even taste the food she ate, and he lacked charm.

But those words and all the rest fled from his head. He could not even remember why he had spent so many days, years, a lifetime on words.

Months spent on a treaty likely to collapse no longer stung.

There was more to life than dry accomplishments that would never please a father who was already dead.

"Miss Snow?"

He knocked upon the door. He didn't even know what he expected to happen.

Listening as hard as he was, he heard her little cry.

Imagining the worst—she had fallen into the fire; the water had scalded her—he pulled open the door.

He'd startled her into throwing a linen cloth over her shoulder, around her body.

It clung like the drapery on marble goddesses. Yet she

stood there, living, breathing. Only his memory of her would be eternal.

She took a step in his direction.

He was terrified of bruising her, or losing her.

Still he couldn't help his long strides to her side, couldn't help brushing the precious curls back from her face, couldn't help cradling her face in two hands so he would believe in her as he kissed her.

The taste of their lips meeting was better than he remembered. Just like the first taste, he knew instantly he wanted more. Her arms wrapped around his neck pulling him down to her, into her. His arms, his hands splayed around her body, her back, held her till he forgot to treat her like crystal and instead she was his delight, his pleasure, his playmate all in one and he crushed her to him, his mouth opening with hers as they explored each other's touches.

Slowly they became two people again, looking into each other's eyes from so small a distance that her face, even her eyes disappeared to him and he felt like he was looking straight at her soul.

"I should go." The part of him that wanted to be honorable.

"Please don't." The living goddess in his arms broke from something eternal into a woman shivering, shuddering, panting as heavily as he. "I've been alone so long."

He became alive to his own even more basic need. He had to keep her warm. He wrapped his arms around her, curved his body around hers. *Please* was the only word he could remember.

But he must have asked if she were cold.

She shook her head, curls dragging along her wet golden skin. "I'm not cold." He looked down; she plucked at his neckcloth with slender fingers. It was true. Heat already flushed through her skin, across her shoulders, down her back, and, as she stepped away and unwrapped the wet linen, across both breasts, their rich curves glowing with fiery color even as her back was to the hearth.

One fold of drapery caught on the pointed tip of a breast, then fell away.

In an instant Victor understood centuries of art that had never interested him before.

Everything about her was so shockingly bare, so alive, so welcoming. He understood the desire to capture an instant like this forever.

But he didn't need it carved in marble. He would never forget.

The moment he thought would never come was here, and it wasn't difficult. It was easy, natural, *right* to catch her against him, to drop kiss after kiss on her hair, her eyelids, her soft lips, her earlobe, her cheek, the sweet skin of her neck.

He feasted there, nibbling, sucking, finally biting her flesh until she made one of those gasping noises and her head fell to the side, giving him the entire feast.

And sighed as he bit her there again, gently, reverently.

Her shivers continued and he wanted more of them. They resulted from the way his tongue traveled upward to the soft behind her ear, the way he nuzzled the edge of her curls, the way his mouth fell again to hers and tasted her there.

He'd worried for so long that this would repel him, yet now with Isabel it drew him. Compelled him. Required him.

His mouth traveled lower, playing with ways of leaving gentle marks on the slope of her shoulder, the swelling skin beneath.

He might have forced himself to stop and look up, to see her face and know if she welcomed his touch or felt overwhelmed; but her hands closed around his face and pulled him lower.

Her breast's red-gold puckered peak was a sweet he had never known he craved. Now he wanted it against his tongue forever. It pebbled tighter from his touch; though he tasted it first most gently, the more he sucked it into his mouth, testing all its textures and flavor, the more she made those sighs till they became a nearly continuous flood of pleasure sounds in which he was drowning.

Inner gates he hadn't known were locked burst open as turned to nip the delicate skin in the crook of her elbow, knelt to kiss the swell of her belly where it began and over its pillowy curve to the cluster of golden curls below.

"Please," he said again; it was all he could say.

She curved over him, protectively, greedily, and whispered into his hair, "I came here for you."

She wanted him.

Her words lit fires in him he had never expected to burn.

* * *

COMPARED TO THIS, Isabel's imagination was pitifully small.

She felt powerful; she felt weak. His touch melted her into softness; she would never let him go.

Every new touch lit fireworks of shock and, yes, embarrassment, touching places she had never expected anyone to touch. Not just touching; kissing, devouring, licking, even to the very core of her where she had never expected to be explored.

His wide hand pulled her thighs close while the other teased apart her curl-covered lips. The cool air in such a delicate place shocked and shivered her, and she had little time to wonder what he would do next.

He licked her there with the eagerness of a man who was seldom indulged and never satisfied.

The pleasure of it pulled her down to him, closer, till she bent over his head, clinging to him to stay upright.

Nothing he did made sense. The slick strength of his tongue in places she had never expected anyone to share, the dip even closer—*inside?*—there was no logic to any of it. Words required logic, order; therefore she could not use them.

Every stroke of his tongue took her higher, pulled her down around him more, shaking under the onslaught of him until everything about her shattered—her last vestiges of reserve, her body, her pleasure, her heart.

Shaking uncontrollably, she fell into his arms, and it was he who gently laid her down.

The possibility of shyness vanished. He stared at her greedily, more satisfied than she had yet seen him. When she tried to fold her knees together, he stopped her with a hand on each, slowly urging them apart again, laying her out in the glow of the firelight in a way that let him see every shivering inch.

"Did you reach the peak?" His voice was rough, urgent. She would have thought him angry had she not already known his emotion was too raw to sound any other way.

"Yes." She had never imagined pleasure like he'd given her. She held out her hand.

He groaned and took it, wrapping his fingers through hers.

Then, "Please?" he said again, as if she would deny him anything, and released her to unfasten his trousers.

Didn't he realize how completely he had captured her? Nothing about her would ever be the same, because now she knew the value of dreaming dreams. "Anything," she told him, and meant it.

Groaning again as if her offer only made him hungrier, he undid the buttons at the front of him and then below those, until he freed a new part of him she had yet to see. It too looked angry, which Isabel understood to mean it too was flooded with hunger and emotions he was struggling to set free.

She expected him to fall upon her; the basic positioning was something she grasped, from somewhere, perhaps a knowledge that floated on the air like clouds.

But he didn't. Instead he took himself in hand and just looked at her.

His eyes and the fierceness in them transformed the last of her feelings from embarrassment to satisfaction. He looked at her. He saw her.

And it was apparently enough to overwhelm him, as with a few strokes of the hardest part of him, four, five, he shot the evidence of his pleasure across her belly, falling upon one hand beside her up-bent knee.

He stared at that, too, with a look of fiercely animal satisfaction.

Breathing hard, harder than when he had carried her water, he bent to press a kiss upon that knee. "Thank you."

He said more with *please* and *thank you* than many a man who talked through supper.

"I did nothing." Truly, she felt more captured than capturing.

"You did everything." He wiped the evidence of his pleasure away with one of the crumpled linens that had been wrapped around her, and Isabel both was grateful for the comfort and sad the evidence was gone.

As if he had something to prove, he staggered to his feet, clearly as weak in the knees from what they had just done as she was.

And then, belying the shakiness he'd just displayed, he took her hands in his, drawing her upright and into his arms again till she floated there, clutched to the hard heat of his chest for too short a moment before he laid her gently down on the velvet-draped bed.

Whatever Isabel expected, it wasn't what happened next.

Victor Adell, Earl of Hartwick for about seventy-two hours, stripped his clothes like a madman, coat flying, waistcoat buttons ripped away, shirt and neckcloth fluttering to the ground until he stood bare before her, matching her openness and vulnerability.

How did his shoulders look even wider when they were bare? Was it the muscle bunching in them as he leaned over her, a hand on either side of her hips, to indulge again his taste for her most sensitive places?

She wanted to wiggle higher to see more of him, but his hand splayed across the softness of her belly held her still. She didn't want to disappoint him. She didn't want him to stop.

The idea of reaching such pleasure once had never occurred to Isabel. Twice was like burning down the world.

The number of things she didn't know seemed infinite as he opened the door to many more. Swollen and sensitive as she was, every touch of his tongue was startling, every inch of her skin had become like ten, all of her wrapping around him and longing for more of him.

If he kept going, the pleasure could kill her.

She would simply have to find out.

CHAPTER 9

$\mathcal{A}$s many times as Victor had imagined enjoying a woman, enjoying Isabel far exceeded every dream he had ever had.

He had never imagined how intimate it would be. Every time he tasted her he felt satisfaction down to his core. Every time she made a gasping moan, it felt like *his*.

His in more ways than one. He pulled those sounds from her. And he felt the same way.

No sound could convey how desperate he was for the feel, the taste, the delight of her. He had felt her shake through the peak of pleasure on his body, on his mouth. He was desperate to feel it again on his fingers, on the core of him. He wanted to feel her ripple around him more than he wanted to breathe.

It was impossible not to rush, even when he wanted every second to last.

Sailors said the night women charged extra for the gifts Isabel was giving him now. She opened her rich thighs to his gaze, to his touch.

It was too incredibly easy to slide one finger into the soft, wet depths of her. He tried two. She writhed in a way he had to see more of; he decided to try three.

The cry she made only drove him into her deeper.

Everything was so soft, so slick, so welcoming. He wanted to explore everything he could feel with his fingertips. There were curves here too, like everywhere on her, little hills and valleys he wanted to map with more exactitude than legal language could specify.

When he curled his fingers toward himself, his glowing, giving Isabel surged upwards, one hand covering her mouth and muffling a scream. Over her fingers, her eyes were wide, shocked.

"Good?"

She nodded. He liked that she didn't seem able to speak.

He would do more of that. He did.

And wonder of wonders, she lost all control.

He had thought he had all of her before. He was wrong. The way she twisted now, gathering fistfuls of the coverlets, writhing her hips against him in blatant, wanton desperation —this was hunger. Satisfaction, too, the satisfaction that all her attention was on him, all her pleasure was for him.

This was everything.

Abandoning her just for a moment to move her till her hips tilted forward over the edge of the bed—she let him do anything he liked—he slid his fingers back inside and this time moaned with her.

He tugged ever so gently on the soft flesh inside, feeling a secret bone curving there, feeling as if he knew things no one else had ever known or would ever get to know about this lavish woman.

He gave in again to his hunger and kissed the swollen nub peeking from her lips.

Fist shoved against her mouth to muffle her own cries,

she curved toward him again with an incredible strength and spent over his hand, his mouth, his life.

He had never even heard of a woman's satisfaction reaching such an extreme. The sailors spoke reverently of being deep inside a woman, but never about this.

Perhaps he had discovered something other men didn't know.

Pride and a dark curling animal satisfaction grew in his belly every time she reached her peak and drew him onward, inward.

He was dying to be inside her.

"Will you have me?"

"Yes," she gasped, this time breathing as hard as if she had been underwater and was desperate for air. "Oh, yes."

It was better than winning a war.

Swiftly he stood, positioning himself between her soft, open thighs and thrusting in.

It was all-encompassing, yes. It was everything sailors talked about. The wet heat pulled at the base of his spine, pulled him forward into her, till he could go no deeper and was forced to retreat.

It was a terrible loss. He recovered by thrusting forward again, willing to fight for his gains, forever if need be.

Each of his strokes seemed to send his delectable woman flying somewhere he could not reach. But he could see it, in the red of her skin, in her open mouth, in her outflung arms. He had caused this. He was making her fly.

Making her his.

For him, every stroke felt like a claiming. Her pleasure spiraled wide while his contracted into the thrust of convinced, determined muscle. He would do this for her forever. He would do this to make her his.

Her gasps grew shorter, higher; she clenched her hands

over her mouth again. He wanted to hear her noises. He wanted to hear her scream.

But more, he wanted to give her everything.

He felt the peak coming, felt the clench of her inside. It was insane how good that felt.

The peak of success.

When she spasmed around him, her grip tight around the white-hot hardness he turned over to her service; when he felt her pouring hot wetness around him again, felt her take him as deeply as she could; he felt that he had given all he could in her service and perhaps had earned his rest.

Gently he held her bent legs against his chest, not letting them go, reveling in the way her bones melted for him, how flushed and peaked he had made her breasts, how spent and gasping he had made her.

With another thrust, another, and another, he felt all the pleasure she had, all she gave, gathering inward from the tips of his fingers to the base of his spine; it exploded there, and the inescapable flood pulled him under.

It pulled him closer to her, pulled him deep. He was under but she was there to welcome him and it was a very welcome drowning.

When his mind cleared, gasping, mouth lax against her soft knee, she still had him in her grip, and she in his. He draped himself over her, wrapped around her, pulling her up into him and against him, forsaking the bed.

He wanted more of her throat. He wanted to feel that fluttering pulse in his tongue. Hungry for so many things he had never even realized he was missing.

He settled for letting her fall back again so he could place a gentle kiss between her magnificent breasts. She looked utterly destroyed, utterly spent.

"You wish to sleep?" He would give her anything she wished right now. Rubies from Persia. Delicate fruits from the Maghreb. Silks from China. She was richer, sweeter, softer than them all, but if she wanted them, she would have them.

She laughed.

Victor had never imagined a laugh like that before either. Helpless, gleeful, innocent and very wicked all at once.

"I cannot stand, much less stay awake," she admitted, while holding out her hand to him again.

Another picture he would remember for the rest of his life. Isabel, flushed and dewy as a peach on a spring morning, golden hair spilling over the linen upon his bed, wicked and sweet and spent.

He kissed the palm of her hand, reveling in her fingertips upon his cheek.

His bones had melted too; he must sleep. But first he fetched one more linen and gently washed her and himself again, dropping the cloths upon the hearth to dry and not burn.

Lifting her against him—another thing he had never imagined; she was so lush, yet so much smaller than he—he pushed the coverlets away and laid her against the sheet, then rolled in beside her.

There was a corner of his mind spinning with facts, and contracts. Marriage contracts, specifically. He had read them but never studied them; now he felt like he needed to dive into all their details.

But first, he repossessed her little hand, and she let him have it.

She touched him so sweetly, and he wound his fingers among hers again even as he pulled her into the space against him for which she seemed made. Once her head settled against his shoulder, he kissed the top of her golden head.

"Thank you," she whispered against his skin, and he

wanted to say so many things, but before he could choose any, a deep dark sleep claimed him.

* * *

It was still dark when Isabel woke from a deep, silent sleep.

Confused at first, she grasped her surroundings piece by piece. A man's arm over her waist. Lord Hartwick.

Damask bed curtains shone dully in the last of the banked firelight. The heavy wood of the house's ancient timbers and floors. The mullioned windows that might once have served princes, looking out over forests of deer, now watching the road to London and smaller houses all around.

Isabel held still and let him sleep, even as she craved his company.

She wanted to peel back the layers of a life with this man in it. She wanted to know him the way her fingertips knew the endpapers of a book. She wanted to lose herself in the colors of his life, in the flowers and silver and satin, of everything he touched, of his skin.

And she knew with more certainty than she had ever known anything before that none of those things would be hers.

Yesterday, *excitement* had meant traveling to a bookshop on her own. Yesterday, if someone had asked her to stretch her imagination, she might have imagined excitement would be a house like this, servants like this, a bed like this next to an ever-burning fire.

Today, excitement was his voice, his body, his eyes, and she wasn't sure if she was blessed or cursed never to have imagined them before.

The gilt edge of the last Lady Hartwick's portrait gleamed in the orange firelight. Isabel was glad she couldn't see the portrait's face.

How presumptuous she had been, imagining any part of him could truly belong to her. She'd spun little daydreams of reading to him, feeding him in her room on Leicester Square. The daydreams embarrassed her now she'd seen the bounty of his kitchen. Unbound by tradition, the servants would feed him as he pleased, better than Isabel ever could.

And what else would lure him to Leicester Square? Her body?

It felt new to her, fresh and unfamiliar and a bit raw all at the same time. She'd heard old women whisper about blood and pain of a woman's first night, but Isabel had none of that.

Lord Hartwick might not even believe he had been her first.

She did not regret. Her daydreams would be richer now, and Isabel was glad of that. She might have died in her little Leicester Square room, years from now, without ever knowing what... all that felt like. Whatever happened now, she would be glad.

Slowly she breathed in and out, fascinated by the feel of his heavy arm around her waist.

Would a night like this have been such astonishing pleasure with any other man? She thought not. Their conversation had been so easy, their secrets, their touch. Easy in a way no evening spent in a parlor with Mr. Ball or Mr. Wheelock had ever been. She had no other experience of earls, but this one was easy to be with, easy to laugh with...

...easy to love.

That was a path she would not take. The very house warned against it. It would be one thing to be a mistress who fed her lord eggs and buttered bread and read him to sleep. It would be quite another to be a lovelorn nightbird weeping at his gates. Even though the house had no gates.

She had no idea what would happen after tonight. He was a risk she'd never expected to take.

She was not suitable for a mistress *or* a wife, but Lord Hartwick was so honorable, so upright, that if there were a child, he would not let it starve. He would see it housed, fed, perhaps even loved. Whatever happened to her, no matter how far she fell, she had only risked herself. Her life. Her love.

A risk she was glad she'd taken.

Isabel told herself sternly—the voice in her head was her mother's—that it was silly even to think of love. She had known the gentleman mere hours. If she grasped one thing about what they had just done, it was that it did not require love.

And the more she thought on it, the more she remembered that he had told her something of his history, his secrets, but had asked very little of hers.

It made perfect sense; he was an educated man of the law, she a brewer's daughter. She had no conversation he'd care to hear. They had met through his chivalry, brusque as it was, not her charm. She was fairly sure she didn't have any.

She had simply lucked into this adventure, a lifetime of memories in one night.

For what could compare to this? Or him?

The sleepy man beside her stirred and made a purring sound and pulled his arm tighter, bringing her closer.

The first time she'd ever indulged herself would likely also be the last. She wouldn't waste this night.

She rolled into him, reveling in the feel of her softness against the hard, furred lines of his body, unable to resist nuzzling the cup of his ear and smelling the scent of him there.

She felt light despite the shortness of their time together, the blood in her veins full of bubbles trying to float away.

But his eyes, when they opened in the deep dark of the bed, were serious.

He surveyed her smile as if studying a letter, put up a hand to stroke his fingers through the wild tangle of her hair. "You are so beautiful."

"So are you," she whispered back, not caring if it sounded foolish to call a man beautiful.

A little frown drew his heavy brows together, and she knew he was confused. He did not think himself beautiful.

Yet he was. From his sleep-tossed hair to the angles of his shoulders and hard-muscled arms, the dips and power of his hips and thighs to the lightly-furred shins and the top of his feet, he was beautiful, every inch of him.

He contradicted her. "I am too thin."

"You are an earl now. Your cook will fill your table with bread and dry beef, if you so desire." She tried to make her voice lightly teasing, as if she wouldn't worry about his table every day for the rest of her life.

He only shook his head, deep dark eyes for once wide with wonder. "How is it you do not judge me?"

Isabel didn't know how to answer. She didn't wish to say aloud that she had only known him for a matter of hours, and if she were in a position to judge anyone she would judge him a fascinating man and a magical lover.

In the dark, their faces inches from one another, he seemed able to say things he otherwise could not. "I never could bear the feel of food in my mouth. Going down my throat. Horrifying. My father called me stupid, he called me weak. Every meal was a battle. Perhaps I won, because he never lowered himself to forcing food in my mouth. Perhaps I lost." He shook his head, looking now into the distance, perhaps at years past. "I find it confusing now. It cannot have been solely rebellion, for I kept to my ways when I traveled. Even when he died." He looked young, and lost. "He died before I could reach him. And I cannot discern if I am sad."

She could not bear the space between them.

Snuggling close into his arms, she buried her face into the space that seemed made for it atop his muscled chest. "Perhaps you *are* sad. Or guilty. Or regretful, or glad. He was not kind."

"No, he wasn't." His arms tightened around her. "Thank you for saying so. Truly I have more regret that I left the treaty unsigned. Though I do regret... I regret that he never cared for me."

In the quiet dark of their luxuriant bed, Isabel's heart broke for him.

"He was not kind—" she felt that understated the truth, but did not wish to say too much above her station, "—but more than that, he was foolish. He wasted all the time he had with his magnificent son. He was a very foolish man."

The truth, or perhaps the startlement of hearing it on her lips, loosened the shadow that clung to him and he laughed, squeezing her close. "Ah," he sighed into her hair, "perhaps I have waited a lifetime for someone to say so."

Satisfied with herself, Isabel pressed closer, and enjoyed the feel in his chest when he made the purring sound again.

"That noise is so unlike you." She could not resist kissing the spot at the base of his throat she had so longed to see. It was indeed strong with muscle and sinew, fascinating hollows calling for her investigation, for her touch. "Hawks do not purr."

"I am not a bird, madame." With one swift motion he rolled above her, keeping his weight on his arms even as he slid slowly, slowly down the length of her body, making her shiver with the feel of every inch of him. Now he was shadowed by the dark of the night, but even so she could see his lazy smile. "I have never felt more like a man. A lucky, lucky man."

Settling his knees between her thighs, which seemed to open for him of their own accord, he pressed himself to the core of her again. Isabel thought she might feel sore, and she did, very slightly, but it faded fast. She swelled again just from the feel of him, the scent of him in the air.

Never in her life had she imagined a man could be so hard and so welcome.

He spoke as if he'd heard her thoughts aloud, answering them. "I never imagined I could feel like this. At peace and hungry at the same time."

She wiggled against him, reaching for the side of the bed. "I recall where to find the kitchen. I could fetch you something to eat."

"I am not hungry for food."

With that he lay full against her, still somehow balancing his weight on arms and knees as if not to crush her, as if he wished to be careful of her.

All at once, Isabel did not want him to be careful.

The years ahead drifted out of sight and she didn't care about them any more. She cared about this, him, tonight, and if he were only hers for one night, she wanted all of him. More of him.

Undulating against him with a wanton thrust of which she would never have suspected herself capable, she slid against him, slick waiting swollen wanting against his matching evidence of desire, and with a groan he obliged her, sliding inside.

He leaned down to kiss her sweetly, warm intoxicating breath like cherries and brandy, but Isabel wanted more. She wanted to be greedy. She wanted to be selfish.

Reaching around his hard body she pulled him into her, thrusting against him with all her might, encouraging him, urging him on, till his groan sounded again, welcome in her ear, and he reached out, seizing her hands and pressing them to the bed in his and plunging into her over and over again, deeper than she had suspected possible.

She only wanted more of him, longer, forever.

They were so shockingly close. No one had ever been closer. Listing the parts of him did no justice to the *feel* of all of him, skin, muscle, blood, everything pulsing against her, *inside* her, making her pulse in rhythm with him.

"Yes," she whispered, feeling she was making too much noise but unable to stay silent.

He made that little purring noise again, more like a growl this time, and muttered into her throat, "Thank you," as if he had waited his whole life to hear her say that one little word.

"Why thank me?" Gasping, nearly laughing, Isabel opened herself to him and gave him everything she wanted him to take.

"I never imagined this," he said again, so serious, his body driving into hers and winding the pleasure tighter, higher, till the heat pooled in her hands and feet like fire and, to the extent she could think at all, she thought she might melt, or explode.

She wanted to keep her eyes open, to look into his, to remember this moment that way, but the inevitable end defeated her, arched her back, bent her neck up to his mouth and closed her eyes as it seized her again in its unforgiving, devouring, devastating pleasure.

When she could breathe, shaking, tears in her eyes for no reason she could fathom, she found him still there in her arms, his kisses touching and stroking her throat, his *yes* and *thank you* storming around her like quiet thunder.

And he stilled too, deep inside her, throbbing, his silent moan against her skin, and dimly she thought he felt how rare this was, how precious.

"Thank you," he breathed heavily, rolling the two of them so she was atop him, banishing her moment of self-conscious nerves with more kisses lighting upon her face, her shoulders like butterfly wings, belying the strength of his relentless grip.

The *thank you* bothered her somehow, as if it had been in return for passing him the butter; but he did not like butter, and if she was sure of one thing, it was that he *did* like what had just passed between them.

"Sshhh." Isabel stroked the side of his face, marveling at the drops of sweat, how hard he had worked for her pleasure, feeling the heat of him subside a little.

And again, he drifted away to sleep.

That must be something men do, thought Isabel as she wiggled away to lay beside him, studying his near-invisible profile in the dark.

It felt so wicked to know what men did in the throes of passion and just after.

A little voice in the back of her mind—and this one sounded like her, not her mother—said that if he woke again, they would do that again, and though she did not believe in old country tales, it seemed obvious that three bouts of such pleasure would trap her here or seal her doom.

She found the chamber pot and used it while counting days. If she was right, her courses would start tomorrow or the next day. They were never very steady.

She didn't know if that meant it was more or less likely that his lordship had given her the ultimate gift for Christmas, but she would have to think about it later. Even a moment devoted to the idea caused such a flood of high and contradicting emotions that she nearly burst out in tears upon the chamber pot.

If she stayed, he would offer her more gifts, or worse, money. There had been too many *thank-you's* to trust otherwise. In the throes of passion, only a man who considered her a peddler would thank her for those wares.

He shifted and lay spread-armed upon the linens, and

Isabel had to ruthlessly crush the urge to crawl back into the bed to lie against him.

She had never ruthlessly crushed anything before. Perhaps it would be a feature of her new life.

For life would be different now. She would never see him again, but her life would forever be divided by this bright shining line: before tonight and after.

Musing that she had never washed so much in her life, avoiding looking at his long, silent sleeping form, Isabel rinsed again, feeling more raw and new than before, then slid into her clothes as quietly as she could, trying not to think about the shock, the heat of his touch. She tied her short stays on over her chemise and rolled her stockings up to her thighs, trying not to think about his touch there. His *lips*, for mercy's sake.

Averting her eyes as she did, she never saw his sleeping hand open and close as it lay on the bed, looking for her.

CHAPTER 10

All the way down the stairs Isabel wrote speeches worthy of any novel to deliver to any servant she saw, but in the end none were needed. Everyone in the house must be asleep.

As she slipped out through the halls, she looked through the paned glass toward the little garden in the center. She had thought there would be time for Lord Hartwick to show it to her, snowy as it was.

But there had been no time at all.

If devastating pleasure put Lord Hartwick to sleep, it acted upon Isabel like coffee. She felt completely awake, conscious of the soles of her shoes against every brick as she descended the stairs, feeling the tie between her and her beautiful man stretching so tight that it was painful but still forcing herself to walk away.

At the kitchen door she paused, laying her hand on the door's frame. Lord Hartwick had a destiny she couldn't share.

But for a few hours, her imagined Lord Mistletoe had been hers.

What's done is done. Her adventure was over. He had a lord's life to live, and she had a room in Leicester Square. They ought never to have crossed paths in the first place.

It certainly wouldn't happen again.

* * *

VICTOR'S LIFE had been a series of uneasy days and uneasy nights.

On Christmas Eve of the year 1814, he slept a long, untroubled sleep.

He woke slowly too, from dreams of clouds as soft and gentle as Isabel's skin, less hungry than usual in his belly and far more hungry for touches and smiles.

Even foggy with sleep, his mind ticked over questions of the marriage contract. He wanted to provide for every day of her future, even days she might have to spend alone. He would provide money, a house, and hopefully heirs who would love their mother and grandmother and great-grandmother. The idea was intoxicating.

Generations of Hartwicks changed because he had fallen in love with a woman.

There was no question in his mind that Isabel was his match, his counterpart. Other barristers might continue to quibble over minutiae once a task was done, but once Victor settled on a correct answer, he did not waver.

Slowly it bore in upon him that his correct answer was not in the room.

He knifed upright. He'd hazily assumed she was behind the privy screen with the chamberpot, but she did not appear, moment after moment after moment.

In seconds he examined every corner of the vast chamber, its dressing room, even its clothes presses.

Isabel was not there.

In a white fury unlike anything that had ever raged through him before, Victor ripped the linen sheet from their bed and, wrapping it around his waist as a modicum of recognition of propriety, threw open the chamber door.

"What have you done with her?" he roared from the balustrade at the top of the steps, a spot that commanded the connection between all the floors. "Did you tear her out of this room? Shove her in a cold carriage on Christmas morning just to spite me? Tell me where you sent her or so help me God, I will dismiss every one of you this moment! I am the earl and *I will not be gainsaid!*"

Servants came running from everywhere, dashing in below wearing crooked livery and aprons that had survived the Christmas Eve revels, and down from above in nightgowns, both men and women.

Including old Mr. Cargill, wisps of white hair jutting out under his nightcap. "My lord, what has happened?"

They all looked entirely too calm. Used to a shouting Hartwick earl, no doubt. That only added fuel to the fire licking upward inside Victor from the vicinity of his heart.

"Miss Snow is not here. Our *guest.* Not a nightbird, a good lady who will one day be—" He cut himself short. His business was none of theirs. "What have you done with her?"

Mr. Cargill still looked too calm for Victor's tastes, but he descended the stairs with the dignity of a man who usually wore faultless coats and organized everything. He addressed the little crowd of startled, murmuring servants. "Who has seen Miss Snow this morning?"

"No one, sir." Mrs. Reed spoke for the bevy of maids, dressed and undressed, who flocked around her. "None of the girls has seen Miss Snow."

"What about you?" Unable to restrain himself, Victor pointed an accusing finger at the lone groomsman who had doubtless been interrupted at breakfast.

"We 'aven't seen no one this morning, sir, an' 'at's the truth." The young man still clutched a Christmas morning apple in his hand, its white flesh showing against the red where he'd bitten it.

"Search the house," was all Victor said and stalked back to his room. *Isabel's* room.

The flurry of noise outside did not penetrate the brittle dome that seemed to settle over Victor with every step he took. He closed the door.

In silence he searched the room again as if looking would produce her. There was no logic in it; he only felt compelled to keep looking.

There was the place where she had lay next to him in the featherbed. There was a slight dip her body had left. There was a golden hair upon the cushions. He could try to keep it, but where?

And he did not want her hair. He wanted her.

There were the linens on the hearth. They were dry now. The spot where she had stood, wet, waiting for him. How long could he live on a memory?

A slight crumble of dirt lay on the hearth to one side. Had she dunked her hems in mud? Her shoes? He imagined her brushing them off, crouching alone at his fire.

Those were the tiny moments that made a life, and he had not paid attention when they happened. He had not known she wore something wet and muddy. It couldn't have happened at the bookshop; perhaps it had happened here, outside his house. His grounds. And he hadn't known.

He hadn't paid attention.

Slowly Victor sat on the edge of the bed where he had discovered Isabel, and delight, and hope all in one night.

Outside the servants still rushed about. They had no reason to lie. They were all well versed in disposing of his father's jolly-girls, to the point of not needing to lie about escorting one from the house, even in the small hours.

Every maid and footman must have heard about Isabel's visit; if the gossip hadn't reached every corner of the house once she sat down at his table, it would have once he confined Mrs. Hopp to her room. They knew to treat Isabel as a guest, not one of his father's servicers.

Isabel had left of her own free will.

The realization spun his mind inward for mistakes he had made, for faults that could have lost him the one thing that had ever been bright. There were so many more than failing to notice her muddy clothes.

Why had he not spoken more about *her* past, her problems? Why had he not insisted on knowing why she, an obviously eligible maiden, walked alone into bookshops in the middle of London? Not to mention travel all the way to his house.

Why had he not asked how she'd done that?

He'd thought her poor from the plainness of her clothes. But he'd met her in a bookshop. Novels came in multiple volumes and could cost ten, fifteen shillings each. Well-bound ones, over a pound. She must have the money to entertain herself if she had planned to buy herself a book, or perhaps several.

She could not have planned to bring unbound pages to his home on Christmas Eve.

It was miles to Allenby's bookshop from here. Her home might be farther yet. How would she get there, if not with his carriage, early on Christmas morning?

Victor was no callow youth. He was trained in the law. His barrister's mind immediately saw evidence of a sharp swindler, probably with an accomplice, one who captured men's attention to get inside their homes and make their theft. An accomplice could have driven her here last night, let her work her wiles upon him, then carried her away again this morning, perhaps with silver candlesticks in her hands.

But it was not possible. Isabel had no wiles. Victor was no judge of women, but he knew maneuvering when he saw it. Isabel did not maneuver.

Somehow she had been delivered to his doorstep, a Christmas miracle, and he had lost her. Because he was a selfish bumbler.

Now that he thought back with his painfully excellent memory, he could remember a thousand moments he could have done differently, and wished he had. He could have told her how lovely she was, how precious. He could have asked about her childhood or her dreams. He could have told her he wanted to wake up with her...

...every day for the rest of his life.

"Mercy help me." Victor, who'd seen precious little mercy in his life, needed it now.

Isabel was gone, he had no idea where.

If his previous days had been bleak, they were nothing compared to the prospect of years to come without her.

* * *

"You're not going out?" Jenny paused elbow-deep in the washtub, agape at the picture of Isabel buttoning her coat.

"I am." Isabel no longer minded being blunt.

"Let me get my coat."

"I'm going alone, Jenny." And before the maid could object, "It's just one of those things we agree not to tell anyone. Just like you leaving early for your Christmas Eve. We can do as we please, can't we? As we are both of age." Isabel's level look said Jenny might well be asked about Isabel's behavior, perhaps at one of her father's pubs, and Jenny could keep such reports to herself.

It was six days since Isabel had arrived home to her empty room frozen and exhausted.

Both the glory of her adventure and the terror of being in the wrong place had dripped away through her toes with every step she took away from Victor and the warm bed in which she'd left him.

With every step panic had grown, whirling between worry that she was already with child and hope that she might be.

London was awash with people who drank her father's ale. A baby meant that someone would find out, her parents would find out, and Isabel would be on the street.

On the other hand, that seemed a small price to pay for the magical gift of Victor's child, a part of Victor who would stay with her always.

Both thoughts had plagued her with every step of the long, cold journey back to Leicester Square. They intruded over and over all through the morning, through Jenny's return, through all Jenny's stories of boisterous Christmas Eve that Isabel didn't really hear at all.

She'd spent a feverish day planning how to present herself at the corner bakery and offer to learn how to sell or make bread.

Then her courses arrived.

Blood was inconvenient enough; now it came with mourning.

For three days she wallowed in sad contemplation that she should be glad there was no evidence of her adventure. Nothing in her room had changed, nothing about her person.

All the changes were inside. She was not the same Isabel.

Now she could say very firmly to Jenny, "I am walking to Allenby's bookshop. I shan't be gone long. In a few hours when I return we'll have dinner."

"But I should—"

"Didn't you say it was bad luck not to finish all the washing on New Year's Eve?"

"Oh yes, mum. Can't wash a thing on New Year's Day, you're washing someone out of your life. Bad luck indeed. But you can't go all that way alone!"

"I can and I will." *I've done it before,* Isabel thought to herself, finding it impossible to explain how she had come by some of the most terrifying and magnificent experiences of her life. "If the washing isn't done when I return, we'll finish it together."

"Oh no, mum!" Jenny straightened, shocked, and soap suds dripped from her fingers into the tub. "That's not work for you, you're a lady!"

"I'm a brewer's daughter and just as capable of washing linens as you." Isabel held back from adding *I'm just a woman.*

She had been raised to think so hard on the differences in people's stations. To capture a place higher than the one where she began, but only by inches. From Victor's arms, the world had seemed much simpler, and much better.

For a few hours Isabel had been simply a person, and love paid no attention to stupidly fine discrepancies.

Jenny and the washing and everything else faded from her mind as she walked down the stairs, already lost in questions that would not be answered by reading.

Had she let her mother's lectures, all those worrying fine discrepancies, lead her away from the luck that had found her, most fortuitously, in a bookshop on Christmas Eve?

In one day's adventure she had discovered so much that she had never known before. Not just the excitement of this house, the trappings of his title, but the warmth of his touch and his desire. She had been desired, and her desire had been returned.

She'd been alive.

On Christmas Day she'd come home to an empty room, still reeling from it all, still convinced she was right. She was no Lady Hartwick. There would never be a floor-to-ceiling portrait of dumpy, dull Isabel Snow. She could no more fit into that world than an elephant could fit a key-hole.

And she would never be a mistress, because there was no Lord Mistletoe. Mistresses had no place in a man's home, and unfortunately Isabel loved Victor Adell, the Earl of Hartwick, with all her heart.

That suspicion grew minute by minute since she'd slipped out of his bed. It had grown into a conviction, and was still growing. It was more intimate than his body inside her, yet more lonely. Something she felt by herself, but was nonetheless very real.

She loved him.

She would not be able to bear news of his marriage to a real Lady Hartwick. Isabel had never been jealous of the women who married Mr. Ball and Mr. Wheelock; indeed, in Mr. Wheelock's case, she felt rather sorry for Mrs. Wheelock.

But the next Lady Hartwick would have not only that ancient house and all the fine things in it. She would have Victor's company, as much as she liked. She would have his conversation, his dinners and his nights. She would have his body and likely his soul and doubtless his heart, for Victor was too honest to marry where he could not love.

Just the thought of it made Isabel burn with envy and fill with tears.

The envy was selfish, a sin; one day she would leave it behind.

The tears were also selfish, sadness for a love found and lost too quick; those would never leave her.

It was warmer on New Year's Eve than it had been the week before, and the paving stones were wet with melting snow as if the world were doing all the crying Isabel could not. Her shoes constantly threatened to slip.

Still she walked toward Allenby's as surely as if she'd been there thousands of times, not just once.

Her journey back from the Hartwick house had taken ages, full of frights and discoveries. Staying away from men, asking direction from the old lady charwomen and fruit sellers who perhaps never needed sleep, Isabel had learned many of the street names, found where to read them, etched overhead fifty or eighty years before. The stones were easily read even in dawning winter light.

By walking south and being brave enough to ask directions, she had found her way home.

She would never be nervous of venturing forth again, because while she could not have Victor Adell, she had herself. And she found that she did not care to spend her life within doors wasting all her future because her past was not what it should have been.

This new Isabel still had the bad habit of correcting others, undoubtedly rude and unwelcome, but she could not fault herself for that when she had committed so many other, greater sins.

Walking along Piccadilly's pavement, she shook her head in admonishment at a stringy boy teasing his sister by holding her rag doll high above her head.

She felt some satisfaction, at least, when he looked somewhat abashed and returned it.

Enough satisfaction to smile just a little, lost in her thoughts, until brought back to earth by nearly colliding with two men arguing nose-to-nose on the pavement right in front of her.

Old Isabel was of course alarmed. Old Isabel was still in her; she could not change that much in the span of a week.

But new Isabel was not so easily scared away. What was

the worst that could happen? Being accosted by a ruffian in a bookshop? Leaving the love of her life?

So she studied both men, one in a fine coat and beaver hat and waving a driving whip, the other stocky, coarse fustian jacket sprinkled with flour.

"No," said Isabel.

Both men stopped, surprised at the interruption.

Isabel took advantage of their attention to say what she thought. "This is not the place to display your bad temper. The rest of us do not need our day ruined by witnessing violence."

Taken aback, the man in the fine hat was used to talking. "This boil-crusted assailant nearly killed me! Ran his cart-wheel into my brougham!"

The miller was slower to speech but more colorfully spoken. "This whey-faced goat-roller is dicked in t' nob! Y' can't drive wherever y' please whenever y' like! Turnt right into me he did!"

Isabel peeked around them both. The vehicles in question stood in the street, blocking the flow of carts and horses, causing many other people to swear just as colorfully as they passed.

Asked the miller, "You were turning on this street?"

"Eagle Street, aye, got a delivery." He jerked his thumb toward his cart, laden with sacks.

She looked up at the man in the beaver hat. He was tall, but not as tall as Victor. "And you did too?"

"Tried to." Past her shoulder, he shook his whip-bearing fist at the miller. "I'll write out a complaint on you today! I have a good solicitor, I'll have you know!"

"I'm sure you have." Isabel still itched to know more about solicitors, barristers, magistrates. Perhaps one day she would. "Did you let him finish the turn before you started?"

"He should have made way!"

"No. How would he know you wished to turn as well? Should he divine it by the way you wear your hat? Imagine if every cart-driver had to guess that others would turn into their path. No one would ever get anywhere."

"'At's right, miss!" the miller shouted in her support.

Isabel held out a quelling hand. "No need to shout."

"I'll show you shouting, you interfering wench! Look at his wagon, not a scratch, and look at the side of my brougham! I demand satisfaction and I will get it." He raised his whip-bearing fist. "Now you mind your own affairs and shove—"

Suddenly the man blanched as pale as the snow.

"Never mind," he muttered and clambered, all whip and limbs, into his brougham as fast as he could go.

The miller stared, open-mouthed, and started to shout something after him; then he too looked Isabel's way. He winced. "Fare-thee-well," was all he said as he climbed up on the seat of his cart and *tch-tched* to the mule to start him rolling.

Isabel wondered for a long second when she had become so frightening.

Then she whirled.

Victor Adell stood behind her, the Earl of Hartwick, all raven-black clothes and glower, the glower fading as she stared, speechless, up into his precious face.

Everything about him transformed. His mouth softened, his remarkable eyes lightened, and he said just as crisply as he said everything, "Madame, I require your help. I have misplaced my wife."

CHAPTER 11

The pieces of his life, so scattered and broken for the past week, slotted together and Victor felt whole again, gazing down at Isabel and all his heart's desire.

She only asked, "How are you here?"

She looked steadier than she had a week ago in a bookshop. It looked well on her. Steadier, but shocked.

He'd asked a question; she had not answered.

But he'd spent six months negotiating a treaty between nations; he could wait much longer for this answer, which for him had more important implications.

So calmly he said, "I walk here every day. You see, my wife ordered several books at this shop." He half-turned and shrugged a shoulder in the direction of Allenby's. "She told them she would return to deliver the books herself, and I dare not risk missing it."

She blinked. It astonished him, how her eyes could be so full of sunlight and snow. He would happily spend the rest of his life contemplating their beauty.

She said, "You paid for the books. I would have seen that you got them."

"I do not want the books. I want you."

Hope, happiness, so many emotions flashed across her face at once that Victor didn't know whether to celebrate or despair. Then her mouth turned down and she looked so sad. "I cannot, your lordship. I *am* sorry."

"Cannot what?" His dreams felt suspended by a thread over a deep, dark chasm.

Fleetingly she glanced around. Passers-by who had stopped to watch the fight between drivers had drifted away, and no one was watching. "I wanted to care for you, Lord Hartwick, I did. But you have *so* many servants. I have nothing to offer."

"Servants are not a wife." The swoop of hope he felt when she said she wanted to care for him, the sinking despair when she said *but*. He hid how the words cut, habitual as it was with him to hide everything he felt.

But that was how he'd lost her once; he could not lose her again.

He moved closer, not to speak in a more intimate way, but because it would offend her less, perhaps, than sweeping her up in his arms and carrying her back to his house, which was what he really wanted to do. "I have never used sweet words before. I have never heard them spoken. But I am good with words, Miss Snow. Please. Let me practice. I will learn."

"I never expected sweet words. Or anything. Not books, or jewels, or coin. You need not fear blackmail or... or a child."

Another swoop of hope, another soul-crushing disappointment. He could not keep surviving them.

Victor had no idea how women knew such things but clearly Isabel spoke only the plain truth. He struggled to find a response that conveyed how he felt the blow, but was determined to put it in its best light. "I can learn new words. But learning to be a father… trust me when I say I've never seen that done either. Perhaps I could not learn something so vast, so all-encompassing. You must have been relieved."

And then his Isabel did something peculiar. She twitched all over, not from nerves, but from some sort of physical urge attempting to win its release. Her whole body shifted, adjusted, her fingers clenched, and he had the impression that were she a sailor from the docks, she would throw a punch.

Finally the burst of emotion worked its way out of her in the tiniest stomp of her foot.

She probably thought her mild scold was a storm of reproach. "You must not speak so. You would be magnificent. I was *so* disappointed."

Victor *was* a quick study. It was obvious that her quiet manner hid vast emotions, much like the ones raging in him. When his Isabel said she was disappointed, the blow must have been crushing.

Isabel stomped her foot again. "We met in a bookshop. We had our Christmas Eve." She pressed a mittened hand to her mouth to stop anything else from coming out, frustrating Victor, who wanted to hear everything she had to say about that endless, glorious night. "It was a stroke of great good luck, but now it is over. There are no consequences. Your life can go on."

Just the prospect of more lonely years without her made his glower return. It was not the right expression for this moment but he could not prevent it. When he leaned closer to speak privately, she did not back away.

"Go on? Without you?" When she nodded a tiny little nod, the pressure in his chest forced out the hardest words. "Did you not notice when I gave you my heart?"

Her mittened hand fell away; her mouth fell open.

"Is there nothing you will not give away as payment?" was what she said.

This was going so badly. They had not found conversing before so difficult.

"I cannot be your mistress." This she whispered. "I simply cannot. Please, Lord Hartwick, do not ask it of me. I cannot do it."

The law had a language, a style. It was not useful for swaying women. For conveying emotion, he had no useful words that were appropriate. Or even true.

Yet law had given him words when his father had not allowed him any.

He must find a way to use them for both their sakes.

Taking her gently by the elbow he turned and walked her back toward Allenby's bookstore, where he had spent six days stalking the pavement back and forth along Piccadilly, looking for any sign of her.

He opened the shop door far enough to ring the bell. "Bring a chair!" he barked inside.

When the shopkeeper came, running and sweating and carrying a three-legged stool, Victor took the stool from him with one hand and closed the door in his face with the other.

He placed the stool carefully so it would not rock and urged Isabel to sit. He knelt beside her, heedless of the wet snow.

People walked past and gave them curious looks, but Victor ignored them.

She had tears in her eyes. He cursed himself for the fool he was. All she really knew about him was his title and his problems. No woman would find that appealing.

When two parties came to the table to negotiate, they came with unspoken assumptions. He had not taken the time to share his or uncover hers. He could treat this as a contract.

Perhaps that would persuade her, for he could not bear to

lose her warmth and wit and sweetness, and all he had to offer in return was a dry, rather battered soul.

"Madame, I have offended you." The evidence was crushingly clear. Her leaving him in the wee hours, her current rebuff.

He would accept if he lost his case, but not without giving his best argument first. Persuasion it must be. He wouldn't beg for her heart; if she gave it, she would give it freely. But he could beg for her hand. If she would marry him, in time, he could persuade her of the love that he was doing such a bad job of showing.

"I can see I asked to be forgiven for my lack of sweet words without making an effort to use any. I cannot erase my failures, because wishes cannot make that so. But let me do better every day for the rest of our lives. Please. Marry me. I may be a poor bargain, but my heart *is* yours. And I want yours in return."

"Oh, God." Now both her mittened hands were clasped into a knot pressed against her mouth. Between the mittens and the trembling rim of her bonnet he barely heard her exclamation and could not tell if it was a prayer or a cry for help.

Either way, he held his position.

Her eyes were huge behind her mittened fists. "You cannot wish to marry me."

Odd retort, but he could manage it. "I assure you I can. I do. That is not the question before us. The question is whether you will."

"You live such a grand life," she whispered.

"I live in offices and ship cabins. My life is not grand. Do you not like the old Hartwick house? I'll burn it down."

"Never! I only meant that you deserve a fine lady. Someone to live your kind of life. All those... things, and places, and people. You must know so many fine people."

He thought of the under-secretary of state who'd invited him to Ghent. The man had lost much of his hair, drank rum when he celebrated, and, Victor happened to know, had crooked feet. "I don't think they are finer than other people."

Now her eyes narrowed a little and he thought she might argue. Argument felt like safer ground.

She did argue a little. "They are, you know they are. They would look down on me like Mrs. Hopp looked down on you. For not keeping things correct. For being wrong."

"And like Mrs. Hopp they would be vile and mistaken."

"You must have such large estates, and ties to government, and so many things I know nothing about and cannot help. You deserve someone born to that world, or at least educated in it. I am nothing you deserve."

"If I deserve anything, it is only what you are. Justice and smiles."

There. He'd found good words. He knew it by the way she looked at him, as if really seeing him. Him, not his suit or his house or his title.

And Victor breathed a little easier, because for the first time he thought he might win.

* * *

Justice and smiles? That was how he saw her?

Isabel wanted to cry and laugh all at once.

She could try to convince him to believe her mother. That Isabel was a dull, dumpy housewife for a curate, yet unable to catch one. That it was the most she could hope for, and having failed at it, she was hopeless. Placeless. Someone who had already wasted her life and was only waiting for death to come.

Or Isabel could believe *him*.

If she believed him... then what?

She had come to London expecting nothing more than to live out her life in a little room watching others out the window.

For the past week her prospects had been no better, but there was an absence there, a hollow wound. Her future was empty and it *ached*.

She had missed him every minute, missed his arms around her as she mourned her chance at his child, missed his frown and his crisp words and the length of his warm, hard body.

Now he was offering her the chance *not* to miss him for the rest of her life.

What if she took it?

Wouldn't it be worth sour looks from a few rigid people? A few mean minutes against hours, years, a lifetime with him? Wasn't there a clear, right answer?

It would only be fair to offer him the chance to reconsider, and Isabel always wanted whatever was fair. "A marriage lasts for a very long time. You ought to be sensible, sir. What if this feeling fades and you repent of your offer a year from now, or five, or ten?"

"Why would I repent?" His knee must be getting cold in the icy snow.

Isabel waved her hands up, urging him to stand back up, but he wouldn't budge. She gave in.

She could not have imagined having this conversation in a private sitting room, much less in public, but if this was where they must have it, she would.

"My lord Hartwick." She met his eyes levelly with her own. "You must know there will be days when you must dine with ministers from Parliament. Or—or rich men who require your work. Perhaps landlords!" That was the grandest thing she could think of. "Your wife should be a Lady Hartwick. Like your mother. Someone who knows how to laugh at the right moments without sounding like a wheezing cow. Someone pretty and smart who can, I don't know, arrange her hair properly."

Something had eased in his face and he no longer looked so desperate and hard. Standing, finally, he paid no heed to the wet stain on his black trousers, only drew her up from the stool and tucked her hand into the crook of his arm.

Isabel tried to ignore how good it felt but couldn't remember why.

"I don't care about styles for ladies' hair. I would prefer a wife to talk as plainly as I do. And my wife will *be* Lady Hartwick. Did someone tell you your laugh sounded like a wheezing cow?"

In fact, her mother had. She remembered that now, as Lord Hartwick maneuvered her through the low door back into the warm dark cave of books.

"Yes," she admitted, "they did. A long time ago. It doesn't matter." Everything before the moment they met seemed a very long time ago.

That dear sharp frown drew his face to an angry point. "It matters. It causes me to wish to commit violence. Odd that only happens in this shop. Here, my man."

He waved to the shopkeeper who, released from the sense that he was not wanted, darted forward again. "I left your chair just outside. My apologies. My wife would like her novels, please."

"Of course, sir. Very good, sir." The man dashed away again.

Isabel ought to let go of Lord Hartwick's hard, steady arm. The urge to keep it reminded her of her urge the week before to find some pleasure for herself. A book all her own. Something to occupy her mind and her days.

What if I did?

Life with this man could occupy her mind and all her days to come.

He could come to regret it ten years hence, but was that not true of every marriage? Were they not all leaps of adventure, like a single woman finding her way to a bookshop alone?

"We barely know one another." She said it quietly while the bookseller's back was turned, ruffling among his volumes. The fellow brought forth a handsomely bound set of one novel then another, piling them upon his table to wrap in rough paper.

"We should repair that." Victor said it so simply. There was not another man in Britain whose mind worked so similarly to hers, however little they knew each other. "My thought was that I would pay proper court. Visit you at home. Speak to your father, of course."

"I live alone."

That made him pause. "Untenable."

"I was—my sister had a better chance of the few eligible bachelors in our village if I was not in view, so my family sent me here."

"Appalling."

"I had my chances at marriage; I simply failed." There, he knew how bad she was at this.

"Excellent." Victor—she must not slip in public, she must call him Lord Hartwick—nodded to the shopkeeper, who tied the twine about their large parcel. "I too have been a social failure. Another way in which we are a good match."

She couldn't bear the thought of him seeing her plain bare room, but it was nothing compared to the idea that she would never see him again.

She drew him away from the seller's table, deeper into the shop. "You should visit. See how simple is my life. And if you change your mind regarding marriage, please still consider me as a possible...lady friend."

"*What?*"

"As long as you do not marry. I admit I could not bear it. Not much good as a mistress, though having met you I was... willing to try. Marriage between two such different people seemed unseemly."

They had just come into the shop; it would be awkward to go outside again so quickly. She saw him think it, marveled that she already knew his expressions so well.

Instead, he escorted her behind one of the taller shelves and for once, mercifully, the shopkeeper left them alone.

"Isabel." His voice was low and urgent and pulled at things inside her that thrummed with excitement at how near he was. "You do not deserve to be a mistress, and I do not deserve to spend days and nights without the woman I love in my house, my bed, my arms."

It still felt difficult to believe. "You are serious."

Slight confusion drew his brows together, those dark hawkish brows. "Am I not always serious?"

His truth was a cliff over which Isabel felt she might fall. "I have just learned to dream. A dream like this is surely dangerous."

He bent his dark head closer to hers. He did not belittle her fears, but he made clear he did not share them. "I never dreamed before either, but now all my dreams are of you."

And as he spoke, his hands slid down her arms, cradling her without cradling her, and wrapped her tensely clasped hands in his. One covering hers, one supporting hers from below.

With him holding her hand, she could take the leap.

She closed her eyes. Could she imagine herself the lady of that Hartwick house, in a dress nearly as fine as the one in his mother's portrait? Directing his housekeeper? Arranging the food on his table, the linens on his bed?

A little voice inside her whispered *why not?*

Had she not been prepared to take care of Mr. Bell's little cottage? Mr. Wheelock's house? Lord Hartwick's house would be larger, but there were also more servants. Even footmen to carry water.

She stopped imagining all the fine lords and ladies who might be there and just imagined him and her. Not as Lord and Lady Hartwick, but as a woman and this man. The man who said he loved her.

That was bracing. She wasn't sure she could be Lady Hartwick.

But being his wife? That would be easy.

His words were already engraved on her heart. *Justice and smiles.* She could do that for him, be that for him, because it was already who she was.

And for Isabel, that settled the question. He wanted her. Just as she was. Exactly the person no one else had ever wanted.

Starting to feel like this might be real, Isabel opened her eyes again to his, watching her. Intently. Waiting.

She did not whisper. "I won't embarrass you?"

She felt as much as saw him settle, no longer stretched so taut. He had been awaiting her answer.

With the utmost calm he drew her even closer. "I believe I will give up being embarrassed. After all, I have done nothing wrong. All that embarasses me now is that I let that evil harridan think she could mistreat me a day longer than she had the right."

"She *never* had the right." If he liked the way she talked, she was ready to do so.

"As you say. I needed the viewpoint of a different pair of eyes to see it clearly. Beautiful eyes like the sun and moon all at once." Offering her his elbow again with a nonchalance she thought he might be feigning, he turned with her to the shelf near them as if perusing the volumes. "And someday if you come to feel a similar affection for me—"

"Oh, I do love you," Isabel interrupted him with unshakeable certainty.

"You do?"

He looked boyish as he turned back to her, heedless of the shop around them or anything else.

"Of course I do. How else?"

"But why?" The Earl of Hartwick looked as confused as she had felt for the last twenty minutes.

That was easy to answer. "Kindness and honesty, of course."

He stared agape at her, astonished, then bent closer. "I would like to seal this bargain with a kiss."

"A bargain? Where you get what?"

"A wife. It is all I require. A wife is a gift, after all, and you the ultimate example."

She thought she saw a small smile cross his lips, the escape of irrepressible joy and unabashed satisfaction, before they came down upon hers and she had to close her eyes again.

His kiss was riveting, taking all her attention, all of her swaying toward him till he stepped as close as it was possible to be and surrounded her in his arms, holding her against him, reminding her that they could yet be closer and promising the pleasure of that again one day.

So this was what dreams tasted like.

And his eyes twinkled at her as he released her, promising her those future joys even as he put her beside him again, her arm looped through hers, and began to speak as if about walks in Wales. "I've contemplated the marriage contract, but had no time this week to draw up any arrangements."

Isabel felt very sure on her feet now. "Why no time?"

"I had to watch the street." He said this as if it were a matter of simple fact.

"Not every day, surely."

He looked at her with his dark, serious eyes. "I have been here every open hour of the shop, looking for you."

Such devotion was unimaginable.

She would not throw such a gift away. Only marvel at it later. Making that much effort, he needed to eat accordingly. She drifted in happy contemplation of planning his meals for the rest of their lives. Dry and simple food, clearly, but much more of it. "You must be hungry."

"Usually," said Lord Hartwick, his finger running down the spine of a book and making Isabel shiver in anticipation, "but at the moment I am quite satisfied."

CHAPTER 12

rue to his word, Victor carried their novels back to
Isabel's room in Leicester Square, and Jenny stood
by with eyes as wide as saucers while he inspected every
corner of the place.

She had never expected so much from Lord Mistletoe,
but Lord Hartwick was unstoppable.

"Mm hmm," he murmured to himself, and Isabel thought
she would be embarrassed, but she was not. He simply was
interested in her lodging.

He turned to Jenny herself with a sweep of his great black
coat. "You have family in London?"

"Yes, sir." The girl hunched her shoulders up toward her
ears. Isabel patted her arm consolingly.

"You report to Miss Snow's parents about her welfare?"

Jenny slunk an apologetic look toward Isabel. "Yes, sir.
Jack at the Iron Cup. I see him every so often and tell him
how it goes."

"And you won't do that anymore."

Jenny looked wide-eyed now, staring at the full glory of

Lord Hartwick. He looked fierce and firm; he required her to make a decision.

"No, sir," she said finally.

"Very good." Crisp and brief as always, he added, "I find I'm in need of a housekeeper, or perhaps head maid, if you are as good at your work as you seem."

"Oh! I know nothing of keeping a fine house like yours must be, sir."

"No?" There was the quick flash of his rare smile. "I think I'd like a home, not a house, and I know nothing of that either, but I'm bound to give it a try. Miss Snow and I will be married very soon."

Eyes even wider now, Jenny clapped her hands and turned to Isabel even as she said, "Yes, sir!"

"Until then I am entrusting her to your care, and Leicester Square." Then, turning to Isabel he added, "Please. I beg you not to walk out alone."

"I have all the books I want now." She pointed to the heap of luxurious volumes piled upon the room's lone chair. "I believe I can limit my walks to the Square for now, if it eases your mind."

"It does. It will. And I shall call each day." Looking about the spare place, Lord Hartwick thrust one gloved hand into his pocket and pulled out a shilling. "Jenny, it is urgent that I see the day's news. Can you find one, perhaps the late edition, sold anywhere about?"

The maid dashed out, coin in hand, and Isabel turned to her Lord Hartwick. So tall and relentless and *hers*. "You did not say during our walk here that you needed a newspaper."

"I didn't. I need a moment alone with my wife."

He swept her up in his arms so fast and so slow at the same time, his movements deliberate yet astonishing, making Isabel's head spin even as he slowly, slowly pressed her closer and closer with both his strong arms and pulled her lips up to his so he could plunder them.

It was a long, slow, lightning-quick time later that she subsided from her toes and breathing again. "We are not yet married," she managed to gasp.

"In my head, we were married on Christmas Eve. More fool me for not saying so. I hope not to exhaust your great store of patience on me before I learn how to live with someone who is not a tyrant."

Her arms floated up to rest upon his before she had time to call them back, and his kisses rained down upon her eyelids, her nose, his caressing cheek resting against hers as he nibbled lower, looking for the spots on her neck that made her gasp and melt.

It must have been quite a while but it seemed no time at all before Jenny came racing and puffing up the stairs. It was easy to hear her long before she opened the door to the little room; Lord Hartwick put Isabel just a hand's breadth away, as deliberately as he did everything, but she saw the fire in his eyes.

It matched the one deep inside her.

He showed no interest in the paper Jenny brandished, her cheeks red from running, so Isabel took it from her, giving him a repressing little shake of her head as she did.

Jenny was no fool.

Isabel couldn't decide if she wanted to ask the maid to make tea or fetch a loaf of bread and see if they could finish what they had started.

It wasn't enough time. She remembered that well.

Victor went on as if they had conversed the entire time about arrangements. "I have no idea where one buys gowns for weddings."

"Nor have I. Please do sit."

He ignored the invitation, staying near her instead.

She skipped her eyes down the front page, looking for something to amuse him. "I don't need a new gown."

"As you please, but I'd like to provide one." He said it mildly and not at all as if he were planning to buy her a dozen finer gowns. "What do you like?"

Yes, she was beginning to grasp the nuances of his brief utterances.

Certainly it wouldn't hurt her to begin life as Lady Hartwick in something nicer. "Perhaps one of the ladies at the bakery will know."

"I'm not interested in the opinion of other women. I would like to know what *you* like." He said it so fiercely that Jenny sidled toward the iron stove to make tea, eyes on him as if he might move suddenly. He kept musing. "Though I have no idea what ladies have in their *trousseau*."

Isabel didn't know what a *trousseau* was. She owned a chest of linens she'd stitched when younger and dreaming of Mr. Bell's cottage; they were at her parents' house. Her sister could have them. The Hartwick family home, she faintly imagined as she studied the columns of newsprint, did not need more linens.

Lord Hartwick was still wondering things aloud. "Of course you'll have Lady Hartwick's jewels, but I would like to find you an appropriate wedding gift. Your taste. Do you like emeralds?"

Isabel, eyes locked on the paper, forgot that she had no idea what a lady should say.

There. Right in the center of the second page. It leaped out at Isabel and caused her to grab her betrothed's arm in a very unladylike fashion.

"Lord Hartwick! Did you see? *Mr. Carroll, a Secretary attached to the American legation, arrived from Ghent yesterday morning with the Treaty of Peace between this country and the United States, and proceeds immediately to Portsmouth to embark on board a frigate for America.* Just look! Look what you've done!"

Finally distracted from wedding gifts, Victor crushed her to him, taking one side of the paper to share it and leaning close to peer at it with his measuring eyes. "Not really. Not *really.*"

"They have! You did! Oh, you brave brilliant man!"

This time he swept her so tightly against him that she was lifted off the floor, and she felt her skirts *whoosh* around them as he spun her in place.

And his few words burst with emotion. "Not wasted! Not wasted after all!"

"Not a waste," she whooped for him. "Not at all."

He'd helped stop a pointless war that he'd hated, helped the women and children he'd met who had made such an impression on him and all the men who deserved justice.

He overflowed with joy, more than she'd ever expected him to show, that his time had not been wasted. That he had done something. That he had helped.

Had Isabel any doubts about joining her future with his, they would have dissolved in that moment. He was so much more than a lord. All the best parts of him no one else would ever see or appreciate the way she did.

"Well done. Oh, well done," she whispered as she slid against him back down to her feet, and this time when his lips found hers she tasted the triumph in them, and smiled against them wondering if she tasted the same way.

Watching maid or no, she would have her lord, and he would have her.

* * *

THEY APPROACHED ST. Martin-in-the-fields on foot, for

exploring the streets of London had become Isabel's favorite pastime, and his lordship always accompanied her.

Usually Jenny followed along as the most desultory of chaperones; today she walked behind Isabel with a basket of little things a bride might require.

"What a busy little nest of streets." Isabel was determined to stay calm, trying to ignore how she'd exchanged her serviceable green wool dress for one of golden silk overlaid with drapings of lace. The lace lay row after row with points that reminded her of snowflakes. The lace had caught her eye and Victor's at the same time.

The delicate double row of emeralds at her neck had been Victor's suggestion but Isabel's choice. She had never felt so grand as she did choosing something worthy of a Lady Harwick. In an hour these jewels would belong to the new one.

Isabel's fingers, in new silk gloves, touched the green stones as she looked up at the church's grand entrance, soaring pillars tucked among the hive of surrounding little buildings.

As always, the grandeur of the place seemed lost on Victor. "I believe there are plans to build a wider street. I do not keep up on London affairs. Ah, Goulburn."

"Lord Hartwick. I had almost despaired of you arriving at your own wedding. Miss Snow." The under-secretary swept off his hat, giving Isabel a deep bow. His high-necked suit fairly burst open at the neck with ruffles; they matched the way he had brushed the hair forward on either side of his gleaming head.

It still made her heart thump with fear that she would say or do the wrong thing before someone important.

But Victor greeted his old friend with such familiarity that Isabel felt nothing could go too far wrong while he was near. "Goulding, have you met Mr. Burroughs? He is here. I asked him to witness our wedding too."

Waiting on the wide stone steps, the sweating bookseller had combed his hair flawlessly, his coat brushed clean, a silk cravat crisp and new at his throat.

He seemed speechless as Victor introduced him to the Under-Secretary of State.

Victor spoke for him. "Mr. Burroughs has done me and my wife invaluable service."

"Pleased." Mr. Goulburn proffered the man a small bow before turning back to Victor. "I've taken the liberty of asking a few more guests."

Victor's fierce frown. "I hope not."

The man seemed to know his friend's moods and, in a kind way, paid them little heed. Isabel had come to recognize that Victor's frown was nearly his default expression; his face simply fell into those lines when he thought, and he thought nearly all the time.

Mr. Goulburn went on with good cheer, "A few of the Ghent men wanted to come. It was a great day, Hartwick, and you were there in spirit. I hope they paint you there, one day when they record it for posterity. You, and me with hair."

Victor's brilliantly joyous laugh came more often now. He clapped his friend upon the shoulder. "Very well. Lead on."

Isabel tried to see the pillars, the grand steps, the vast glowing space inside the church the way Victor did, as a collection of shapes and light, nothing more important than that. Tried to feel as though the dark-coated collection of people inside on this January morning were simply people, not ministers of state and—gracious—likely a few lords and ladies too.

But some of them likely were lords and ladies, and Isabel had no one to invite except Jenny and some ladies from the bakery.

She had not wanted her father, mother, or sister there; she planned to inform them of the wedding by note. Next week. Perhaps the week after. There was no rush.

They had not wanted her in their lives; she did not want them in hers.

Then Isabel saw someone with her feet in both worlds. Lady Arnold, the widow who lived on a southern corner of the square and the bakery's patron, oversaw many of the comings and goings on Leicester Square. Isabel had seen her, perhaps spoken to her twice. It was beyond kind of her to come; Isabel couldn't even be sure how she knew.

The lady clasped Isabel's hands in hers as Victor accepted salutations from some of his colleagues.

"The most important wedding is in your heart," she whispered, as if they were friends, as if Isabel let Jenny take off her walking coat.

Then her ladyship pressed a small posy of mistletoe and two rare yellow tulips into Isabel's hand.

Tulips, in the dead of winter.

Isabel felt her shaking heart settle.

In a dress fine enough to suit any Lady Hartwick, Isabel walked step by step with Victor down the aisle to the waiting archdeacon of London, whose fine robes—*oh my*—brushed the floor, but who also had kind eyes and a gentle silver fringe of hair.

The archdeacon smiled at Isabel as she approached, as if he expected her, as if she belonged there, with Jenny and Lady Arnold beside her and Mr. Goulburn and Mr. Burroughs next to Victor Adell, Earl of Hartwick.

Her husband.

The preliminaries of the ceremony washed over Isabel unheard, occupied as she was with her unaccustomed finery, people's kindness, the grandness of the otherwise empty church, and most of all the firmness of Victor's solid arm under her hand.

Victor spoke often of the legalities of the ceremony. He'd purchased a common license, arranged for the church of the parish in which she lived, cemented every detail as if he expected their marriage to be challenged in court. If it were, the challenge would lose.

She had not expected the awe-inspiring sweetness of this moment, or the clearing of the archdeacon's throat as he paused.

When she looked at the grand clergyman, framed by the carved plaster ceilings of the elaborate church, she thought she saw him blushing a little.

He turned his book to a loose, inserted page. "In younger days I was foolish enough to pen a few verses, and I promise that I do not include them in marriage ceremonies as a rule. In this case, his lordship made a request."

Then he read in his fine voice:

"Oh fairest beam of heavenly light
That lead'st the starry train of night;
Calm silence smooths thy tranquil way,
And pensive Sorrow loves thy ray.
And when you reign, the shadowy train
Of fairy footsteps mark the plan;
And dimly, by thy beams serene,
The ghosts of lovers oft are seen.
You wished to say something, Lord Hartwick?"

Victor cleared his throat too, as if making space for words.

He turned and looked down at Isabel, never more fierce than now in his fierce love.

"I wanted to borrow words that would convey that you are my daylight and my night. I know nothing of poetry, yet now I can imagine how past lovers felt because it must have been like we do. I hope many other lovers yet to live can be as happy as I am, as happy as I hope to make you."

She had not imagined how he could make her heart melt.

* * *

THE WAY ISABEL looked up at him—adoring, sweet, so very glad to be here with him—was all Victor needed. The way she spoke when they were alone, through each walk and during stolen evening kisses, of the things she'd seen, the things she thought, filled places in him he hadn't known were empty.

All he wanted was to listen to her talk to him for the rest of their lives.

He had not expected her to speak aloud, shy as she was except when something was unjust.

But she did have words, and they surprised him.

"You taught me to dream of a better life. Dreams aren't selfish. I understand that now. Dreams are all that separate hopeless lives from hopeful ones. If I can help you spread any of the hope—the *joy*—you've taught me to feel, it will be a life well spent. I thank you, Lord Hartwick, for all the gifts you've already given, and for all the gifts to come."

And with that, his fellow lawmen from Ghent gave a little cheer. Rowdy they were not, yet they felt moved to express the solidarity of their emotion.

Overcome by unfamiliar feelings of recognition, support, and most of all joy, Victor ever afterward remembered, first and foremost, the things she said and then the feeling of sliding the cool gold ring on her finger.

That and her sigh of relief once they crossed the threshold again, shouted good wishes behind them fading in the morning light.

His carriage stood closest to the door, crowding the street, Mr. Bottle holding the reins.

Someone had decorated the Hartwick carriage with yew branches, more mistletoe, and red ribbons.

Victor nodded at the driver, who tipped his hat and bowed a little with an easy, "Lord Hartwick. Lady Hartwick."

The last vestiges of Victor's tension faded away.

He'd spent so much time in Leicester Square this last week, getting to know his bride and ensuring her safety, he had left the Hartwick house to stew in its own juices, as it were.

Isabel had visited the house with him twice to arrange their chambers, tell the cook her tastes, and once, with Jenny falling asleep on a chaise in a corner, to read Mrs. Burney's latest novel together late into the night.

All he had requested for today was to order the wedding breakfast, knowing Mrs. Reed would manage it.

Now the decorations felt welcoming, as if the entire house might welcome home its lord and new lady.

It warmed him as he settled into the seat next to his wife.

Perhaps he had overestimated others' hostility. Trained as he had been to see viciousness everywhere, he had perhaps not noticed how many people did not subscribe to it.

His father and the odious Mrs. Hopp had loomed so large in his life he had perhaps failed to notice that others did not agree. *Peculiar,* he thought as he settled in beside Isabel's warmth and braced his arm behind her so she would not be jostled too badly by the movement of the carriage. One or two evil people caused so much havoc, and their removal so much peace.

Like Napoleon, he thought, reminded of the emperor banished to his little island. Perhaps evil people ought to know *their* place.

Regardless, his wife and their future was much more interesting.

He squeezed Isabel's hand now. "For all our wanderings this week we have not walked as far as the Hartwick house. I still cannot imagine you walking such a distance yourself."

"I only did it once," she confided. "A carriage driver took me there, the first time; I only walked home."

"Is that so? What carriage?"

"A hackney. The one that took you."

"The same one?"

"The very same. I recognized his face. You would too if you saw him; he had those red cheeks, and a red hat."

Victor could not recall seeing any such gentleman. "How much did he charge you?"

"He wouldn't let me pay at all. He assumed you were my husband, said you would pay when we reached home. I fretted about it the whole way, then once we reached your house he only said I should be home on Christmas Eve and drove away."

"And so you were."

"It wasn't my home *then*."

"It was waiting to be." Which was the simple truth. For though at the time he had only been Earl of Hartwick for mere days, he had been waiting for that house to be a home all his life, and what that required was Isabel. It always had, and it always would. "*I* was waiting to be. Never has a pantomime turned real so quickly as my pretense to be your husband in that bookshop."

"The hackney driver thought you were my husband because I let you kiss me." She leaned into his shoulder. He loved the sensation.

"Perhaps he thought me your husband because of the way you followed me to the carriage," teased Victor back.

Teasing was not a skill that came easily to him, but he was learning. It took trust.

"I think he just wanted to help me. He knew I needed help."

"I needed it too." Settling back into the seat, Victor cushioned his wife's journey by pulling her closer with his arm, supporting her with his body, his strength. He ate more these days, knowing his right to whatever food suited him, and being far, far less hungry in his soul. "What a bear I was that day."

"You had already done something great. You just didn't know it yet. Imagine, they signed the treaty that very Christmas Eve, and you didn't know. Signed by the King the day before New Year's eve, and you had to read about it in the paper." Isabel looked indignant, his favorite judge. "One of those gentlemen might have written you a note."

There was nothing so pleasant as her righteousness on his behalf. Victor shrugged, enjoying how it pressed her softness into him. "Perhaps they did. There is a prodigious amount of correspondence upon my desk at home."

"And you paid it no attention?"

"I was busy walking up and down Piccadilly looking for my wife." He reached over to play with the fingers of her far hand. "And how do you like your ring?"

Just as he knew she would, Isabel drew off the ring to examine it closely from all angles, as she did everything.

He saw the moment she spotted the engraving in the weak January light. Saw her read the words he'd put there.

Justice and smiles Christmas Eve, 1814

She nodded. When she looked up at him again, he thought he saw a tear at the corner of one eye.

He kissed it away.

"I have a gift for you too." Drawing up the little basket Jenny had thrust into her hands after she settled in the carriage, she drew out something the size of a letter. He unwrapped it from its length of linen.

It was a stitching sampler, simple and beautiful, like her. On a stretched, framed scrap of green wool—no doubt a remainder of the dress she had worn the day they met—she had embroidered white Christmas roses in mistletoe, and three words.

Kindness and honesty

He felt his mouth pursing and twisting, trying to discover a new shape to express all this joy.

"Is it too simple?" She leaned into him to study it in his hands, which he enjoyed for multiple reasons. "Ought it to have the Hartwick crest on it, or...?"

"It is perfect. One cannot improve perfection."

Taking him at his word, Isabel nodded and subsided, then, before he could miss her warmth and softness, wrapped her arms around his arm and pulled it close.

As the houses thinned, Victor began planning how to shorten the time between giving up their pleasantly close position in the carriage and taking up a similar one in their house.

At least Isabel looked as sorry as he felt when their carriage finally rolled to a stop.

Then her face changed as he handed her out at the base of the ancient steps, which were lined with all the Hartwick servants on both sides, all the way up to the door.

EPILOGUE

*I*sabel nearly dove back into the carriage.

The line of servants was overwhelming. All so crisp and straight and staring at her as she emerged from the carriage. Not Victor, her. Dull, dumpy Isabel Snow.

No. She took a deep breath and straightened her back, correcting herself as bluntly as she did others. *I am not Isabel Snow. I am Isabel Adell, Lady Hartwick.*

It was true, and she must bear up to it.

But every step she took toward the brick-lined path felt lighter and lighter. There was Mrs. Reed at the head, all smiles and a fat lace cap, and Mr. Cargill's strict face nearly cracked with an actual smile.

"Lady Hartwick." Mrs. Reed curtsied.

"Lady Hartwick." Mr. Cargill bowed.

"Her ladyship does not wish to greet all the servants now, it's been a long morning," said Victor with his usual direct simplicity.

"But I do wish to greet them!" Rushing to speak before the moment passed, Isabel looked at them all, even if it was too hard to see them in the glory of all the finery they'd donned to honor her and their lord's wedding. "I am so very grateful to all of you for meeting us like this. I feel very welcome."

She felt more than heard the pleased little rustle. As if acknowledging silently among themselves that it would be all right, this new business of having a lady of the house.

"That's right, my lady, you'll talk to everyone, but not today." Mrs. Reed let Mr. Cargill lead the way between the double row of servants, then, as Victor would not yield his place beside his wife, followed just a step behind. "I've made your wedding breakfast, if you don't have any more guests."

The latter she said with some suspicion, as if Isabel and Victor would start producing guests from their pockets.

"I hadn't realized there would be any at the church," Victor told her without much interest.

"They cheered his lordship aloud," Isabel confided over her shoulder, squeezing her husband's arm as she walked.

"Of course they did! I hope you'll want to give them dinner one day, my lady." Mrs. Reed sounded a little wistful, as if delighted by the prospect of cooking a large meal. "This morning, I only wanted to know where you wanted break-fast served."

Isabel looked toward Victor, but he only said, "Whatever you like."

Panic threatened to sweep over her at the thought of having to decide, the worry of doing it *wrong*, but she shook her head and shook it away. "No, this is *our* breakfast. And we have been here so little. I'd like to know where you prefer to eat."

"Hidden in my room," he said with that dry flash of humor that she loved so much.

"Tut." Mrs. Reed hadn't approved of Victor's plans to make the chamber where he'd been living into a bedroom for both him and his wife. It was unseemly, and there was too little dressing space for two people.

Nonetheless, she had carried out Victor's wishes.

"I like that." Isabel looked over the lawn at the house toward the window she'd first seen from within. "At that window there? We will do that."

"Yes, madam." And Mrs. Reed cut across the snowy lawn with a flurry of crunching footsteps to get to the door first.

As they followed her in and climbed the stairs to the room where they had spent their fateful Christmas Eve, Isabel learned why Mrs. Reed had hurried. She ushered a little parade of footmen and maids, all trying to look unflustered, up the stairs. They marched in and out of the grand chamber quickly before Victor drew her in and locked the door.

Not one but three little serving tables sat by the sweeping many-paned window. One held fresh bread, apples, a cutting board with a silver knife, and a wedge of yellow cheese from Cheddar. Plain sliced ham and beef were arranged on a little serving rack above a silver platter so every piece of meat had stayed dry.

But another held a gold-rimmed porcelain cup with boiled egg, honey, a fat tub of butter, a silver pot of bracing hot chocolate, sugar-iced biscuits, gleaming amber orange marmalade, and a delicate plate of sauced prawns with the scent of herbs and lemon.

The third table held a dish of sugared almonds and a collection of plates and cups, as if she and Victor might wish to trade bites of the dishes so obviously set for them. It also held a carefully pressed newspaper. The morning edition.

"All this for us?" asked Isabel in wonder, her fingertips balancing on the handle of the silver pot, as she turned back and looked at him over her shoulder, one bright curl falling to her shoulder and a lifetime of smiles waiting on her lips.

* * *

He would have her painted one day, just like this, Victor thought. Just like this, with the gentle glow of the glass window illuminating her, picking out every glittering detail of the lace on her gown, none of which shone as bright as her eyes looking at him with obvious, delicious love.

"This should be your portrait." His throat felt thick; he had to swallow. "The new Lady Hartwick in her home."

That was when Isabel looked around and noticed that the vast portrait of his mother was gone. "But where is your mother's portrait?"

"Elsewhere." Victor was hungry, but more for her than food. She was determined he should eat; he would never waver on his feet again from hunger, but he might fall down to his knees in entreaty. "Till the new Lady Hartwick decides where it should go."

"But where *ought* it go?"

"Anywhere. The nursery, if we have children. My mother would like to be in a room with our children, I think."

"No. Children throw oatmeal mush," ruled Isabel with that delightful certainty.

"It's an oil painting. It will survive."

He couldn't last a moment longer without offering her something to eat. She nibbled the biscuit he handed her, a sparkling crystal of sugar taunting him from her lips until he kissed it away.

She smiled as she looked up at him. "I think I would prefer to be painted with my husband, if anyone paints me at all."

"I would be happy to arrange it, Lady Hartwick. That and any other presents you wish."

"My birthday is not until May," she said with a teasing

sweetness, shaking her head as if denying he would give her more gifts.

"I've grown very fond of Christmas, myself." Gathering her softness into his arms, he pulled her a little closer; gladly she came. That soft sweet warmth he might have missed, but for a bookshop and the kindness of a stranger. "I may start to keep Christmas all year round."

* * *

WANT *a little bonus time with our mistletoe lovers?*

Get a glimpse of their trip when they finally make it to Wales - and join the world of romance by Judith Lynne!

HISTORICAL NOTE:

Allenby's is of course based on the glorious Hatchard's, which has been on Piccadilly since 1797, so they say, and has served many royal households. I have imagined its interior from images of other bookshops of the time, as it had not yet grown into the glorious temple of books that it is today.

Interestingly, it was nowhere near as large as the actual Temple of the Muses, which sold vast quantities of ready-made books at cheaper prices, but not on credit. The Temple's owner Mr. Lackington, previously an illiterate shoemaker, served humanity when he worked with a few others to publish an odd little book in 1818 called *Frankenstein*. His store had large areas for reading and relaxing, as Isabel and Victor tried to do at Allenby's that fateful Christmas Eve. That store appeared as a most secret meeting place in *The Clandestine Countess*.

The Treaty of Ghent ended a painful war between Great Britain and the United States in which little was accomplished except the deaths of many men. Among other issues,

Britain wished to keep impressing American men onto its ships, treating the United States as a vassal nation despite its independence; Americans, as one might expect, did not want that. The end of that war marked the beginning of a new era of international law—and the beginning of the end of similarly treating the Native American nations who also participated in the war. Different Native American nations allied with the British in the north and with the Americans in the South; none of them received any of the sovereign lands that they were promised. Victor's vision of international law came into fruition, but not for indigenous peoples. So there is always more work to do.

For a view of the likelihood of commoners marrying peers, which is much more likely in this period than anyone might suspect, I am indebted to David Thomas' article "The Social Origins of Marriage Partners of the British Peerage in the Eighteenth and Nineteenth Centuries" in *Population Studies* (vol. 26, no. 1, 1972, pp. 99–111. JSTOR, https://doi.org/10. 2307/2172802). JSTOR is an international treasure and of inestimable value to private researchers like me.

AFTERWORD AND
ACKNOWLEDGEMENTS

For this book I must first and foremost thank my readers, who were so patient with me for *months* while the title of this book was revised, and revised, and revised again. Poor Isabel looks lovely next to Hartwick Hall, but spent far too many weeks without her title.

It was you, my readers, who convinced me to keep up the search for a much better title; and I thank you for both your inspiration and your support.

It seems to be a peculiar feature of my books that I am inspired to write love stories about people intimately involved in the hidden details of history.

The Treaty of Ghent didn't interest me at all, till I imagined what would be happening around Christmastime 1814 - well after the events we are following for the Maids Done Waiting (and a few other stories yet to come).

My repressed, slightly prickly new lord wound up being a lawyer. Unattractive, you may say; yet how valuable they can be.

This led me into a little study, not just of the difference between barristers and solicitors (so fascinating to the American mind who has no daily interaction with them), but also diplomats, and the recording of history.

The signing of the treaty was indeed later painted, and Mr. Goulburn was indeed painted with hair. (You may note that this flattered him, from his depiction in other portraits.)

Please forgive me for placing Isabel's rented room between the Ladies' Own Bakery and the boarding house of girls in trades; my heart is never far from Leicester Square, and the third season of LOB begins soon.

A NEW SERIES BEGINS:
MAIDS DONE WAITING

Lady Viola has little regard for family; hers never cared for her. None of them, not even her brother the physician, ever helped her through her bouts of melancholy.

She'll be damned if she'll leave the Duchess' court to wait on her now-widowed mother.

No, she'll be *married*.

Desperate for the shelter of marriage, Viola must hurry and kidnap herself a husband.

Lee Waite has returned from wandering England's wilder corners, finally healed from the war. He's ready to marry someone sturdy enough to withstand the winds of fate. That doesn't describe his best friend's delicate, determined sister. She's a creature of the heights of society, which never welcomed him; and he knows better than anyone that her brother's a crack shot.

Once captured, Waite must see to Lady Viola's safety. The more each learns about what the other has survived, the closer they come.

And the more desperate he is to escape her lord trap before she learns what kind of a man she's captured.

* * *

The Duchess of Talbourne's maids in waiting (*What a Duchess Does*) will finally find love! Lady Viola's story kicks off this set; these are MAIDS DONE WAITING. Stay tuned for Virginia's Happily Ever After!

2024 nominee for the Maggie Award for Best Historical Romance, Georgia Romance Writers

* * *

Read The Lord Trap *today!*

ABOUT THE AUTHOR

Judith Lynne writes rule-breaking romances with love around every corner. Her characters tend to have deep convictions, electric pleasures, and, sometimes, weaponry.

She loves to write stories where characters are shaken by life, shaken down to their core, put out their hand…and love is there.

A history nerd with too many degrees, Judith Lynne lives in that other paradise, Ohio, with a truly adorable spouse, an apartment-sized domestic jungle, and a misgendered turtle. A past writer of SF and screenplays, she pens Regency romances of love you can believe in, with a rich sense of place and time.

If you enjoyed Lady Mistletoe by Midnight, *help keep these books coming - share a review at your favorite bookstore, Bookbub, or Goodreads!*

Sign up for the author's newsletter, including exclusive book news and sneak peeks,
at judithlynne.com.

ALSO BY JUDITH LYNNE

Lords and Undefeated Ladies

Not Like a Lady

The Countess Invention

What a Duchess Does

Crown of Hearts

She Tamed the Lady *Forthcoming*

He Stole the Lady

No Titled Lady *Series prequel*

Lady Mistletoe by Midnight (*Standalone novella*)

Maids Done Waiting

The Lord Trap

The Lady Escape *Forthcoming*

Cloaks and Countesses

The Caped Countess

The Clandestine Countess

The Curious Countess (Novella)

The Castaway Countess *Forthcoming*

Ladies' Own Bakery

Ladies' Own Bakery Season One: The Collected Episodes

Ladies' Own Bakery Season Two: The Collected Episodes